NOBODY IS EVER MISSING.

ANDERSON V. BERNARD

This is a work of fiction. The events and characters described herein are imaginary and are not intended to refer to specific places or living persons. The opinions expressed in this text are solely the opinions of the author and do not represent the opinions or thoughts of the publisher. The author has represented and warranted full ownership and/or legal right to publish all the materials in this book.

'Harvested'

Nobody Is Ever Missing.

All Rights Reserved.

Copyright © 2020 Anderson V. Bernard

This book may not be reproduced, transmitted, or stored in whole or in part by any means, including graphic, electronic, or mechanical without the express written consent of the author except in the case of brief quotations embodied in critical articles and reviews.

For Emmitt, for Trayvon, for George, for Breonna, for Tamir, for Ahmaud, for Eric, for Mike, for Vanessa, and all the other wonderful souls stolen at the hands of evil in America since 1619.

For the stolen and missing souls.

Across the world.

America and the world has a missing person's problem. Watching your local evening news, and when reading current events on your favorite social media sites, you come across thousands of missing persons' pictures, some, who are never to be heard from, or seen again. What becomes of those individuals? Are they just gone forever? Why did they go missing in the first place, and what entities are responsible for their disappearance?

More than 600,000 people go missing each year in the United States according to The National Missing and Unidentified Persons System. There were 40,000 cases of unidentified remains and 1,000 of them were from the Delaware valley. Of that 600,000 in the United States of America, 64,000 were African American women, and children who were declared missing in the year 2019. As of February 18th 2019, Pennsylvania had 401 open missing persons' cases, which was the tenth highest in the country.

What are we supposed to do when we hear those staggering numbers? What are we to do about young children murdered mysteriously and found with their internal organs removed? What is going on? Who should be held accountable? Are people being stolen? Are human body parts being harvested?

(The above stated number facts are true. This novel is a work of fiction. A.V.B)

HARVESTED

CENTER CITY PHILADELPHIA Pa. 2019
2:07 a.m.

"THANK YOU for coming out...God bless you, goodnight!"

The club bouncer shouted and instructed the party going crowd to exit through the nearest doors. The security guards opened side doors and welcomed the warm summer breezes to the delight of the sweaty party goers. The overhead lights came up, shining on the club goers who scurried towards their friends and personal belongings as they started to exit. Young twenty something's, men and women, brushed past one another, some with sweated out hair and others with beaded sweat covered brows. Miniskirts and blouses perspiration dampened, and t-shirt armpits soiled way past moist. Crumpled liquor stained napkins, half empty drink glasses and beer bottles covered the bar top, and the smell of spilled liquor fumigated the warm breeze and blended with hints of rank body odor, sweated out perfume and cologne.

"You aint got`ta go home, but you gotta` get the hell outta here!"

The bouncer repeatedly shouted louder and louder as he pointed toward the exit doors. The three bar attendants cleaned, and wiped the bar top removing items, tossing everything in a nearby trashcan. Melody and her two friends met near the table where they`d been sitting and drinking most of the night. Melody locked arms with her girlfriend Vicky as they strolled off the dance floor away from the two guys they`d spent the final five songs of the night twerking with. They wobbled their way toward the table where Fiona was seated holding their purses. Melody was wearing her favorite form fitting black skirt that gripped her full hips perfectly. Her Tupac t-shirt was sweated completely out in the arm pits and her curled black weave hair was now pulled back into a scruffy damp bun. Vicky had beads of sweat shimmering all over her skin and her peach fuzz reddish hair edges. Her crop top help perspiration at the bottom and she carried her black heels in her hand after taking them off on the dance floor two songs in.

"And look at these two thots. Sweaty, and drunk. Who raised you hoes?"

"Don't be a hater Fi, we got it in for you tonight," Melody slurred giggling.

"Somebody had to drive tonight, it was your turn," Vicky slurred.

"The club was definitely lit tonight," Fiona said as she passed her friends a bottle of water each.

"Drink up hoes...let`s go get breakfast food...I'm starving."

Fiona interlocked her arm into Vicky`s and the three women strolled out of the club arm in arm blending in with the exiting crowd under the sound of the club security repeatedly shouting exit instructions. The three friends strolled toward the parking garage down the block and were met with shouts from men leaving the club.

"Where y`all going?" shouted an inebriated bald guy.

"The after party is at my crib," yelled a chubby dark-skinned dude.

Melody turned toward the guys and shouted back.

"The after party is at the breakfast hut!"

"Shhh! Why the heck you telling them where we`re going?"

"Girl you talk too much when you get turnt," belted Vicky covering Melody`s mouth.

"Yesss, now if they show up, they gonna be in our faces, expecting," Fiona preached.

"Y`all hoes shut it, they might buy our waffles too," Melody advised giggling.

The three friends shared a laugh as they walked to the parking lot.

"Greedy ass," Fiona mumbled as she held onto Melody tightly…

St. Louis Missouri
12: 07 am.

Candice finished her shift at Missouri medical center hospital. She said good night to the third shift desk attendant and strolled through the automatic door. Her energy was low after working a double shift but she always kept her polite continence with the hospital staff.

"Hey Candice, have a good night…drive safe now."

"Thank you Rod, I`ll, see you tomorrow…and, time to quit smoking Rodney."

"I`m try`na sis, fa`sho, this is my last year," Rodney stated as he finished puffing his cigarette while standing under the overhang out of the drift of the misting rain.

"Okay now, I'm gonna hold you to that."

"You want me to walk you to your car?"

"No, thank you…I'm just across under the light," Candice stated as she pulled her hooded rain smock over her head and waived.

"Alright then!" Rodney shouted. "Wit`cha juicy bubble," he whispered under his breath as he gazed at Candice's' ass poking through her scrubs as she strolled away.

Candace walked down the path away from Rodney headed toward the street parking in front of the hospital. She made her way across the two-lane highway and walked toward her car parked along the hedges on the other side of the roadway. Candice pulled her hood back so she could see clearly and then pulled mace from her purse and flipped the cap open. She grabbed her car keys from her pouch and pushed the ignition car key between her middle and ring finger and made a tight fist. All the things she'd remember from her self-defense class. She looked left then right as she made her way to her car. She opened the car door with her key, relaxed and jumped in. She pulled her hood off, shut the door and started the car turning the windshield defrost and heat on low…

Camden N.J

2:15 am

Clay always chose to make his scrap metal runs late at night. He knew his competition would delay until the early part of the morning on trash day to look for scrap metals in the garbage piles. Clay drove his already half full pickup truck slowly down Beckett Street. He pulled to a stop and exited his truck. He walked to the curbside in front of a home that had a large pile of mangled metal shelving. Clay pulled the metal from the trash and tossed the pieces into the rear of his truck underneath an old refrigerator door he'd collected earlier. He climbed back into his truck and started a slow cruise down the block looking left and right at the trash piles. He drove to the corner of the street and noticed an old stove. He pulled to a stop and jumped from his truck. He looked at the stove and tried to lift it. He struggled a few feet and sat it down unable to wrap his arms completely around it. He took a few deep breaths and lifted it again dragging it barely off the ground. He managed to shove it to the rear of his truck and stopped the stove at the rear lift gate on his truck. Clay climbed into the back of his truck and grabbed to large straps and tied them under the stove. He knotted them and then pulled them over top of the stove. Clay climbed into the rear of his truck and started pulling the stove upward into the rear of his truck. As he struggled, he noticed a midsized unmarked moving van driving slowly toward him with the head lights out…

Philadelphia Pa.

3:45 am

    Fiona made her way back to her white jeep after dropping Vicky and Melody off at their apartment. Vicky watched out the front window from the fourth floor as Fiona walked up to her car. Fiona waved bye as she reached the passenger side door and Vicky waived back and closed the window blinds. Fiona looked at her driver side mirror and saw what looked like a white handkerchief tied around her mirror. She hesitated and looked around checking her surroundings. She pulled the handkerchief off her mirror undoing the tight knot with both hands.

    "What the fuck is this?"

As Fiona finished her sentence, she undid the knot and threw the handkerchief to the ground beside her truck. Fiona lifted her red skirt slightly in front and raised her car remote. The handkerchief floated to the ground and Fiona hit the unlock button on her jeep. She pulled at the door handle and felt a sudden sharp stinging on the top of her left foot.

"Ouch, shit!" Fiona swore as she jumped backward away from her jeep.

Fiona looked down at the top of her open toed shoe and saw an arm and hand pulling away from her foot quickly. She panicked and backed away from her jeep slowly. She saw a hypodermic needle stuck in the top of her foot with the plunger pushed all the way down. Her heart started racing as she moved away gradually bending over looking under her jeep trying to get a clearer view. As her fear level arose a shadowy figure rolled from under her jeep wearing an all-black jumpsuit with a black ski mask and hood. The shadowy figure climbed to his feet and stood unmoving. Fiona fixed her lips to scream but nothing came out of her mouth. Her head started spinning and her stomach evacuated all the food she had eaten at late breakfast. As she backed away slowly her brain told her feet to run but she couldn't move. Her eyes moved in the direction she wanted to run, but her feet didn't respond. Fiona bent herself over at the waist and struggled to pull the hypodermic needle from her foot. Her toned arms and hands felt weak and flimsy. She got hold of the needle and tossed it to the ground as she vomited again. Terrified, she staggered away a few more feet further from the shadowy figure, looked around, and fumbled her purse and keys. Again, she thought to scream out. Her mind clouded with a fog and she could hear her own thoughts blasting loudly in her head as she looked up at the apartment window of Vicky and Melody. *"Run Fiona…Scream Fiona…fight Fiona."* Her body didn't respond. The stranger strolled to pick up the needle and then started moving toward her leisurely. Fiona fell to the ground delirious and clumsily rifled through her purse grabbing at her cell phone. She stood again but her legs became uncontrollably weighty and couldn't hold her upright. She crumbled back to the ground just as the shadowy figure reached her. Her eyes blurred and glossed over as the figure lifted her from the ground. Fiona dropped her phone and tried to struggle and fight swinging her arms. They cascaded off the shoulders and face of the stranger and fell flimsily at her sides like over-cooked spaghetti noodles. A midsized unmarked moving van pulled up next to Fiona and the assailant. The rear doors flung open. Two more figures jumped from the van dressed in black jumpsuits and lifted Fiona's body into the van. The doors on the van shut quickly leaving Fiona's keys and purse on the ground next to her jeep and cell phone…

St. Louis Missouri

12:10 am

Candice turned her car radio on and turned the volume up on the quiet storm slow jams she loved listening to on her drive home. She warmed her car for a few more minutes and then turned on her windshield wipers. She sat for a second waiting for the blades to clear her windshield of rain mist. The blades moved half an inch up the windshield and stopped.

"What the?" Candice mumbled.

Candice turned the wipers off, then on again. The wipers moved half an inch up the windshield and stopped again. Candice exited her car and moved to the front hood leaning overlooking at the windshield. Her wiper blades were zip tied together preventing them from moving across the windshield. Candice pulled her hood back over her head and yanked on the zip ties trying to break them apart. She looked around checking her surroundings and yanked on the zip ties again trying not to break her wipers.

"WHAT THE HELL!" Candice exclaimed.

A midsized unmarked moving van pulled up beside Candice and stopped as she pulled on the zip ties. The passenger side window rolled down and a voice called from the window.

"You okay there miss…car trouble?"

Candice turned around quickly at the sound of the voice. She was startled because she never heard the van pull up behind her as she focused on the zip ties.

"Somebody put a zip tie on my blades," Candice groaned desperately.

"What? Maybe I can help you with that."

The man exited the passenger side of the van and Candice looked him up then down. Candice peered into the driver's seat and saw the dark silhouette of the driver. The dome light in the van never turned on inside and Candice noticed the headlights on the front of the truck were off. The tall stranger approached Candice never making eye contact with her.

"A zip tie you say?"

"Yes…why would somebody do that," Candice asked stepping a few paces backward from the stranger while pointing at her wind shield. Candice examined the black jumpsuit and skull cap. Her heart started racing and she balled her fists while thinking of her keys that were in the ignition. Her mace was inside the car in her purse. Her instincts screamed threat in her gut. She took a step rearward and tried to pull her car door between herself and the stranger. The stranger smiled at Candice and quickly pulled a taser from his pocket and rushed Candice. He pushed the taser against the chest of Candice who tried to jump out of the way. Candice chopped at the strangers' arm and threw two punches landing flush on the strangers' face. The stranger absorbed the blows but kept rushing forward slamming the open car door. The taser landed solid against Candice`s chest just as she landed a hard knee thrust to the ribs of the stranger. The taser sparked brightly in the mist and rain and Candice flopped to the ground shaking from the voltage blast with her fists still balled up and swinging in midair. The assailant lost his wind from the knee thrust and buckled slightly. The driver's side door on the van opened up and the two men rushed over and quickly lifted Candice from the ground and put her in the rear of the truck. Her rain smock was still smoking in the front where the taser hit. They locked the door on Candice's car leaving the engine running and drove away in a matter of seconds…

Camden N.J

2:19 am

Clay pulled hard on the stove while keeping his eyes focused on the van that was now diagonally beside the rear of his pick-up. He made sure that his stove find was on the rear of his truck before what he thought was his competition in the parked van, could make some kind of bogus claim. He`d heard it all before. He was on the west side one late night, early morning and he came across another junk scrapper who asked Clay, "*What the hell you doin`wurkin`my neighborhood?*" Clay spent the next few minutes fist fighting that man for an old metal cabinet and a pile of mangled shelving cabinets.

"Need a hand over there big man?" a voice asked.

Clay muscled his stove onto the lift gate of his truck and dragged it into the rear across the bed. He undid the straps quickly as he peered into the passenger side of the van where the voice came from.

"Don't need help friend, thanks just the same," Clay responded defensively.

Clay gazed at the van straining to see inside. Clay climbed out the rear of his truck and grabbed his crowbar and stood holding it. He waited for a response from the motionless van. Nothing moved.

"I`m good`ere, don't need help!" Clay boasted defiantly repeating himself.

A few seconds passed. Clay stood his ground looking around the area and at the truck. Clay shut the rear of his pick-up gate slamming it shut and walked slowly toward the driver's side door holding his crowbar. He looked over his shoulder at the truck that was just sitting with the engine running. It was running but Clay could barely hear the motor which was strange for a moving truck vehicle of that size. As Clay reached the side of his truck, he heard the rear of the van doors unlock and saw them swing open. Two men jumped from the rear of the van wearing black jumpsuits and ski-masks. Two more men jumped from the drivers and passengers' seats and started aggressively toward Clay. Clay started to retreat quickly with his crowbar in his hand tightly. The four men rushed toward Clay. The man from the passenger side of the truck pulled a pistol taser from his jumpsuit and pointed it at Clay. He fired the taser and it hit Clay in his stomach and the voltage sparked against Clay`s body but barely penetrated his insulated coveralls. Clay swiped at the tentacles of the taser wires and struggled to keep his feet while backing up in a state of distress. He stumbled rearward and yanked the taser tentacles` from his body.

"Hey, Hey Got Dammit!" Clay shouted angrily. "What- is – this - shit?"

The driver from the truck pulled his taser and fired it at Clay hitting him in his chest. The four men rushed Clay grappling trying to subdue him. Clay swung his crowbar forcefully and struck one of the men in the head. The heavy thud landed flush on the strangers' cranium sending a hollow echo into the air. The stranger was dazed from the blow and instantly crumbled to the ground. Clay then pulled his pistol from his coverall pocket quickly and fired two shots from his trembling right hand. The shots stunned the attackers' momentarily who never saw the gun. One of the shots landed by chance in the face of one of the strangers who fell to the ground bleeding from his head. The other two men desperately tackled Clay knocking the pistol and crowbar from his hands. The driver blasted Clay with another burst of voltage from the taser. Clay wriggled on the ground like a fish out of water while reaching for his gun.

"Enough with the taser, don't burn the skin!" One of the assailants shouted.

The shouting assailant quickly kicked Clay in his head twice knocking him unconscious. The dazed assailant climbed to his feet and the three men lifted Clay from the ground and carried him to the rear of the truck and rolled him inside. They snatched the wires from his torso and scurried back toward their fourth member who was dead and lifted his body, grabbed the revolver pistol and tossed the dead assailant into the rear of the van and shut the doors. Two men scrambled to the front of the van and pulled off quickly as they removed their ski masks. The van sped away down Beckett Street as lights started turning on in bedroom windows and living rooms in the row homes.

St. Louis Missouri

12:15 am

Candice's body was rolled inside the rear of the midsized type moving van. The inside of the van was totally dark. The only light illuminating inside was from the green neon lamp sticks worn around the necks of the strangers in black jumpsuits.

"Remove her garments quickly," a voice urged from the deepest part of the van.

Two strangers quickly ran razor sharp scissors the length of Candice's body from shoulder to feet tearing her rain smock and scrubs away. They pulled her garments from under her and then cut away her underwear leaving her smooth toned physique bare.

"Perfect specimen…and she's a fighter." the voice groveled. "Everyone, I'd like you to meet the true mother of civilization," the surgeon said gazing at Candice's naked body.

The cutters and handlers looked on.

"Perfection…Here before your very eye is the ONLY scientifically known organ that possesses the mitochondria DNA, that contains ALL variations possible for every different kind of HUMAN- being- on -earth. The black woman's DNA can mutate into ALL others…this- is- EVE. The genes are only found in the black woman."

"Profoundly interesting," responded one of the garment cutters after a brief moment of silence.

Candice moaned lightly and started to move her head.

"Get her into the bunks and administer ten milligrams of propofol while we prepare the surgery."

The two garment cutters lifted Candice from the floor of the van and slid her body onto a foldout bunk that was bolted to the inside panel of the truck. They placed her body on the bottom bunk. On the top three bunks were three other bodies stacked to the top. Three other African American women were covered in white blankets and strapped neatly into the bunks with heavy leather straps. They were connected to intravenous propofol drips that rendered them unconscious. On the other side of the truck where four other bunks filled with African American men, covered in white blankets, and hooked to IV propofol drips. Candice moaned again loudly.

"Quickly, and gently…we don't want her awake."

The two garment cutters strapped Candice into the bunk and carefully needled her arm and connected an IV. They turned the drip on quickly and Candice passed out seconds after. The instructor moved from the center of the darkness and pressed a switch in the top part of the truck.

Light illuminated the center area of the truck and from wall to wall inside, the truck looked like a hospital emergency trauma center room mixed with the lab of an evil scientist. There were two medium sized see through refrigerators filled with dozens of quarts of blood, and large jars filled with formaldehyde with different internal organs floating inside the jars. The floor had splatters of blood spilled about, bloodied gauze piles in one corner, and a large metal autopsy table in the center where the groveled voice surgeon took a seat and started looking at a small electronic tablet. Each one of the bodies in the bunks were connected to its own digital read out of vital signs that were attached to the side of each bunk on a miniature computer screen. The instructor moved deliberately past each tablet and read the vital signs. He then moved back to his chair area and focused on his personal tablet.

"Candice Sanders, aged twenty-seven, athletic build, African American woman, perfect condition," the surgeon spoke into the open-ended microphone on his tablet. He stood to his feet placing the tablet on his chair and pulled a black smock from a locker behind his chair. He tied the smock behind his back and dressed his face with a surgical mask. His tablet chirped loudly and he picked it up and read instructions from the screen.

"We are to remove the kidneys; lungs, liver, and heart for immediate processing…get a bone marrow kit, and take tissue and blood samples for further experiments…secure the remaining corpse for bleaching and melanin removal procedure in four hours once we return to base."

The two garment cutters unhooked Candice from the bunk and carried her body over to the narrow table and carefully placed her down. They pulled her feet apart strapping them to the bottoms of the tables and did the same to her arms. Candice's` body was stretched across the table like a four-point star fish. Her dark brown skin rippled from the dampness and temperature inside the van. The garment cutters connected her IV to a hanging metal clasp in the roof of the van. The graveled voice surgeon grabbed a bone cutting saw. He turned the saw on and it vibrated loudly. He turned on a small concentrated overhead lamp and leaned in over Candice's body. He turned the saw to a higher speed and Candice opened her eyes and moaned.

"Dammit!" screamed the instructor. "Is she under ten Milligrams?"

"Ten exactly sir," responded a female garment cutter.

"Well administer five more, plus five of morphine, she`s obviously stronger and heavier than we thought and needs a higher dosage," the instructor scolded.

"Yes sir," responded a male garment cutter.

"We need to go quickly, we have clients in need," added the surgeon as he plunged the saw into the chest cavity of the woozy Candice. Candice convulsed from the pain of the saw and moaned loudly as the saw penetrated her flesh and quickly cracked her chest plate. Blood splattered into the air as the female garment cutter quickly added the extra millimeters of propofol and morphine into the IV as the instructor had ordered. Candice's` body jerked a few seconds as the saw blade cut her from her clavicle to her breast area sending more blood spraying into the air. As the propofol entered her bloodstream her body relaxed onto the table. The instructor waited a few seconds for her blood to collect around the cut and pool itself on the table bottom and drain beneath into a filter under the table. He made another quick cutting motion into her breast area and pulled her chest cavity apart. Her ribs made a loud cracking sound that reverberated inside the van. He moved the saw downward against her navel area and cut through toward her pelvic area and the table flooded with blood. He grabbed a pair of clamps and handed then to the female garment cutter. Candice`s heart muscle was exposed and beating and her lungs were inflating and deflating in the open air.

"Kidneys' first," he mumbled through his mask as the female garment cutter secured her mask around her face and clamped at the kidneys'.

"We remove the heart last…Kidneys', liver, lungs, and heart. In that order."

"Yes sir," the male garment cutter said as he prepared large jars filled with formaldehydes.

Town and Country Missouri

Saturday 9:30 am

Saul Walthers was sitting outside on his patio watching landscapers work on the over grown trees behind his estate. He read his morning newspaper, sipped his coffee and scanned his laptop for current events in the news. His patio doors opened and his wife Katie made her way gingerly through the doors on a walking stroller accompanied by a nurses' aide who was close behind. Katie walked slowly toward the table breathing heavily with a portable oxygen tank over her shoulder. Saul stood and smiled. He kissed his wife on her forehead as she took her seat at the table.

"Great job," the nurse aide insisted.

"Thank you, Janette."

"You`re welcomed…I'll get your breakfast Katie."

"Thanks Janette," whispered Katie. "Can you put just a little butter on my toast…please?"

"No butter Katie, you know better," Saul advised. "No butter Janette."

Janette smiled a half smile at Katie and mouthed the word sorry as she walked away.

"You're feeling better today…I can tell by looking at you."

"Yes…I slept well last night…there wasn't much snoring going on."

Saul broke into laughter and Katie laughed as best she could while catching air from her breathing tank.

"I'm sorry darling, I'll do better," Saul said smiling.

"Are you going to the building today?"

"No…I'm staying at home today with my lovely wife. Sugarland IT is running itself today…I figure, you, me and Janette should go visit the grandchildren and shop for clothes and toys."

"Spoiling my grand babies is always a good thing," Katie said smiling.

Janette rushed through the patio doors with a look of fright and excitement on her face. She was holding a silver pager in her hands that was continuously beeping a loud piercing sound. Katie looked at Janette in disbelief and Saul dropped his paper on the table.

"Saul?"

"Janette is that -"

"I was making the toast and it started blaring…it's the hospital," Janette belted interjecting nervously.

"Oh my God," Saul said reaching for his cell phone.

Katie sat still watching with nervous intension and Janette sat next to her as Saul called the hospital. Once Saul connected to the hospital the pager stopped resounding. The phone call lasted close to a minute with Saul doing most of the listening. Saul hung up his cell phone and gazed at Katie with an astonished look on his face.

"Katie, we need to get to the hospital as soon as possible…they found a heart, and it's yours my darling," Saul gushed exuberantly.

Philadelphia Pa.

4:10 am

Fiona's body was strapped to the center of a cold autopsy type table in the center area of the van. Four people moved about the van reading vital signs of people strapped into metal bunks that lined the sides of the van and were stacked like bookshelves. Seven racks, filled with human cargo. Fiona's body was naked. Her caramel skinned torso was covered with maker lines in the shape of a large Y that started on her left and right shoulders, connected at center between her full breasts and straight down the center of her body through her pierced navel area stopping at the top of her vagina. The instructor examined Fiona's body and skin closely. He rolled her back onto the left side and looked at her back examining her spine, then made his way around the table and did the same to her right side as he fingered her smooth skin gently.

"She is a grade 'A' capture," the female instructor commented.

"Fiona Middleton aged twenty-two," stated a stranger dressed in a black smock and mask.

The female instructor motioned the busy group to the table and the four other strangers dressed in black garments gathered around the body.

"We saw directly along these lines, adding extra pressure at the breast plate to break through. We gently cut beneath the flesh, peeling back the skin gently as not to damage it. Once there, we pull away the fatty tissue protecting the organs. Then we extract the major organs. Once inside, we cut and clamp what we need. This Y cut direction allows us to remove and reach every part, and remove rib bones if needed. This body is supreme. The immaculate skin tells us everything…limited alcohol consumption in her young life, non-smoker, and athletic tone in the muscles, the long healthy dark brown hair and the breasts. The hips and lips are firm and full…very fertile specimen here."

The group looked on and listened to the instructor as she pointed through her descriptions. Fiona blinked her eyes and started moving her head. She tried lifting her head slightly and was held down by one of the male strangers in the black smock. Fiona opened her groggy eyes and tried to focus as her heart started racing and she started breathing rapidly.

"Hi sweetheart," the female instructor whispered leaning over. "You can relax, we are taking you to the hospital…you are going to be just fine."

Fiona relaxed onto the table with heavy eyes and a soft smile of relief. She relaxed her breathing. One of the men in black connected an IV to her arm.

"No propofol…a dose of morphine to put her under, and for the possible pain…we are using everything on this one. After we remove the major organs, we remove marrow, stem cells, the remaining blood for immediate processing, muscle tissue, the brain and skin," noted the instructor.

The instructor put on a pair of surgical gloves as the others in black strapped Fiona's body to the table and hooked IV's to both her feet, and another to her arm. The morphine entered Fiona's body and two minutes later the instructor started the saw. The loud buzzing startled Fiona slightly awake. She peered through sleepy eyes at the instructor who smiled down at her. The instructor waited another five seconds and Fiona shut her eyes again. Her body went numb on the table. The instructor started cutting along the Y as Fiona's chest cavity was still moving. As the instructor pressed the saw, the moving van hit a deep pothole in the roadway and the entire van jolted. The instructors hand shook hard and the saw slipped slightly.

"Damn it!" shouted the instructor. "Pay attention to the road."

The instructor finished sawing through the skin and flesh of Fiona carefully for twenty more minutes. When she was finished Fiona's torso was filleted and open on the autopsy table like a gutted fish. The instructor pushed her hands into the cavity and moved Fiona's intestines' outside her mid-section and reached the right kidney. The instructor looked around at the others in the van who were paying close attention. The instructor pressed down on the edge of the kidney and used a scalpel to cut it from the body. One of the garment cutters took it and carefully placed it in a jar of formaldehyde. The instructor moved the intestinal organs to the other side of the cavity and removed the other Kidney. The instructor made clamp after clamp, and cut after cut, until Fiona's body cavity was nearly empty. The blood drained under the body and into a filter that pumped it directly into large empty saline bags. Twenty more minutes passed and the instructor was still working. Fiona's heart was still beating and pumping what was left of the blood remaining in her body. The instructor extended her hand and was handed three large clamps. She snapped the clamps in place and cut the ventricles of Fiona's heart. She clamped twice more and then removed the heart muscle while it continued beating. It was placed carefully into a separate medical container and quickly placed into a refrigerated cabinet. The instructor stepped away from the table and sat down covered in Fiona's blood.

"Close the body, staples only. Shave the hair at the scalp…Get the heart to our recipient ASAP… We're done for tonight," affirmed the instructor.

University of Medicine Center Hospital

Philadelphia Pa.

The operating room was lit with bright overhead lights. The surgeon was connecting the second kidney inside of twenty-three-year-old Sarah Lansing. The nurses and attending surgeons watched as the doctor started closing the wound. Doctor Goldenbaum paused and motioned his attending surgeon to finish closing. He passed the attending doctor his utensils' and instructed the close…

Doctor Goldenbaum entered the family patient care waiting area. The Lansing family, Alton Lansing, his wife Emily and their son Erving were seated in lounge chairs watching television. Alton Lansing stood to his feet as the doctor strolled into the room. Emily examined the doctors' face closely and interlocked her fingers under her chin in anticipation.

"It went very smooth. No problems at all. The second kidney seems to be taking very well, and she should be out of harm's way in a couple of days."

Emily let out a sigh of relief and Erving smiled.

"Thank God…and thank you for everything you've done doctor."

"You're very welcome Mr. Lansing. We do our very best for our patients here at Center hospital, especially for our esteemed board members, and business owners like you. Thank you for your generous donations to our institution here over the years."

Alton Lansing smiled at the doctor and shook his hand.

"How long before we can see her?"

"She's being situated in her private room as we speak. Twenty minutes. She'll still be a bit sedated and in need of rest…room 220."

"Thank you doctor…any chance of these organs failing?"

"Well…we happened to secure these organs from a principal donor within the city limits… whom was just about the same age as Sarah and in superb conditioning. They should work out fine."

"This principal donor donated both kidneys?" asked Emily Lansing.

"Mrs. Lansing, I'm not really at liberty to discuss issues of this matter in detail, but yes, the person passed away suddenly and donated all of their organs."

"Grace and mercy…Alton, we have to do something for that girls' family."

"No, no, that won't be necessary, you and Mr. Lansing are not supposed to know…consider yourselves blessed."

Philadelphia Pa.

One week later

4090 Delaware Avenue 7:00 pm

The Old Richmond power station sat vacant near the Delaware River factory area for years. In its hay day during the 1920's, the station was the work horse for the majority of the electric power being produced in Philadelphia Pennsylvania. The large industrial building with solid stone seventy-foot walls rested just off the pier area. The structure was one story and the concrete walls were ten feet high all around. The outside walls were a dirty tan color and had not been painted since the plant closed its doors in 1984. The top of the structure had large windows on all sides that were shaped like half-moons. The inside of the plant had five-inch-thick steel walls covering the plant on all sides. The floor of the plant was all concrete and steel with seven large electrical generators in the center of the space that stretched clear through to the ceiling. The rafters of the building looked as if a giant spider had spun steel webbed arches in all directions connecting the beams across the top.

Six unmarked midsized moving vans were parked in the rear of the station in a row near the loading dock garage doors. The outside of the building was fenced in with new fifteen-foot-high chain linked fencing that was woven with dark green plastic strips to block viewing from the outside. The chain linked fencing had razor wire around the top and security cameras on the outside of the building and along the fencing. There was one sign on the front entrance gates of the fencing that simply read "Building Under Construction."

Several cars were parked in the lot near the vans and several more arrived at the gates where several security guards checked each car for proper identification prior to entering. Men and women dressed normally exited cars and entered the side door of the building…

A few feet behind the largest unused electrical generator sat rows of chairs. The chairs faced a make shift podium with four seats on it and a large screen projector behind it. The four seats were occupied by three men and a woman. The gentleman in the first seat stood to his feet and the soft chatter in the room subsided.

The screen behind the man lit up with graphics in a pie chart. The States around the country started to appear in alphabetical order. In each state an accounted number appeared next to every state and city name with the word 'Harvested' next to it. New Jersey had 37 next to it, fifteen from Camden. Missouri had the number 42 next to it, 22 from St. Louis. As the audience irrupted in soft claps and cheers at the numbers running on screen as the states rolled by, several people dressed in black shirts and jeans passed out small pamphlets to the rows.

The first gentleman moved to the microphone and waited for the clapping to end completely. He absorbed the applause conceitedly.

"As we can unmistakably distinguish, our efforts are coming along significantly…but, let us not celebrate until we reach our desired numbers for the year 2035. We still have a long way to go…great work everyone…now a word from the director."

The speaker walked to his seat and a thin man moved to the front of the podium wearing a dark mask over his face that was shear but distorted his appearance enough that his real features were askew. The rows applauded exultantly as he reached the microphone. He raised both of his arms to the side with his palms up and open. The applause level rose higher in volume. The sleeves on his tight black blazer moved up his wrists. The room echoed louder and stopped as he dropped his arms and adjusted his jacket. The thin stranger looked over the area at the men and women seated in segregated sections by colored armbands worn on their right sleeves. One group wore black, another red, and the final two, white and blue.

"BROTHERS and Sisters…We`eee are the keepers and controllers of our earth!" the thin man boasted proudly. "We`eee must maintain, preserve and safeguard our position…We can on`nnly accomplish that by perfecting the immense work we are committing right now…there`s copious numbers of progress to be completed, and mistakes to be corrected…upon examining your documents you will see that our networks are growing. We have added a list of funeral directors who have establishments ready to accommodate captures and process them with and for us…the principal matter at hand, we are losing people in our efforts, and this is unacceptable…We are the captors, not the victims…from this moment on, we raise the numbers on collecting specific women and children only, particularly those of African descent, as their parts and the melanin they carry are of the`ee greatest value…The adults collected thus far are superb, but now, more recently the adults are arming themselves in record numbers and are killing our comrades…We – Can - Not – Have – This!…We`ve lost several associates because of this in recent events…It`s the children and women to be collected from this point on, until further notice," instructed the thin man as the audience sat still and listening attentively.

...

Noah sat on the sofa in his mother's living room watching the evening news and eating a large bowl of chocolate puffs cereal.

"Mah'ma… it's on again," Noah shouted.

His mother Pamela hurried through the pathway from the kitchen at a quick pace headed toward the television and stood next to the sofa and looked on. The evening news was broadcasting a segment about a missing young woman, Fiona Renee Gilliam from West Oak Lane.

"There she go mah' looking all ratchet," Noah taunted, pointing out his sister Melody on the news broadcast.

The news broadcast was taking place at the Oak lane court apartments where Fiona went missing and her truck was found. Every branch of local news was there with a reporter and cameras filming live. There was a large group of people from the complex and surrounding homes watching as the Gilliam's` made their plea for help with finding their missing daughter.

"I saw it earlier boy…and shut up and get your feet off my coffee table," Pamela stressed in an annoyed tone.

"Weave tracks looking dry," mumbled Noah under his breath with a mouth full of cereal.

Pamela slapped Noah in the back of his head.

"Why are you eating cereal when I'm cooking dinner? And go put a shirt on…When your sister gets here, I don't want no mess. She`s going through enough with Fiona being missing…so don't add your…your foolish shenanigans, not this evening Noah."

Noah sat his half-eaten bowl on the coffee table and strolled out of the room.

"Get this bowl Noah…take it into the kitchen."

"I`m not done with my snack mah…I'm gonna eat it."

Pamela glanced at the television and walked back toward the kitchen shaking her head with frustration as Noah darted up the steps skipping two at a time.

"I mean it," shouted Pamela. "When Mel gets here you be extra nice," she added shouting upward into the ceiling of the walk way. Pamela reached the kitchen moved around the area anxiously lifting pot lids and apprehensively checking food in the oven. She paced and mumbled under her breath for several minutes. She finally paused and sat at the kitchen table with a look of despair on her face.

...

"Mah, it's like she just vanished into thin air. Her car was still outside the apartment where we parked," Melody explained emotionally.

Pamela and Noah sat staring at Melody from across the small kitchen table and listening as they ate dinner.

"Me and Vicky got up the next day wondering why her car was still there…Vicky was the one who went to the car and called her cell. That's when she heard the cell phone ring coming from under the truck."

"That's really so sad Melody, I'm so sorry your friend is missing, she is such a wonderful girl."

"Don't worry Mel…she gonna be found safe."

Melody forked around in her mixed vegetables and wiped at her swollen eyes with her free hand. She felt good about the verbal love she was getting from her brother, and especially her mother.

"I just don't understand why this is happening…like this."

"Try and eat your food Mel, you`ll feel better."

Awkward silence lingered in the room for a few seconds as everyone focused on their plates.

"Did you see yourself on the news, that weave track right there was sticking up like a California palm tree," Noah joked teasingly pointing at his sister's hair.

Pamela cringed and snarled at Noah. Melody lowered her head and cracked a momentary smile through her gloomy face, and then laughed calmly while rolling her eyes at her younger brother.

"You soooo stupid," Melody replied to Noah laughing softly. "Goofball."

"I know how to make my sister smile."

"That news interview was strange…it was like, nobody really cared that Fi is missing, they were just out there doing a job recording stuff and that's it."

"They are just doing their jobs baby…don't get angry at them."

"Mom, they were jostling at Mr. and Mrs. Gilliam trying to get the best emotional T.V. clip they could…it was bizarre and annoying because I could tell the Gilliam's are overwhelmed, being from Jamaica, their daughter is missing, and nobody has answers…it was heartbreaking," Melody quavered as she started to rupture emotionally.

Pamela began tearing up at the sight of her daughter emotionally out of order. It evoked bad memories of past hardships from her relationship with her daughter. Pamela folded her hands under her chin and shut her teary eyes. Noah got up from his seat and quickly kissed his mother's forehead. He then walked to Melody and wrapped his arms around Melody from the back and held her tightly as she cried.

"It's gonna be cool sis, they gonna find her…no worries."

Melody stood up from the table and walked out of the kitchen wiping back her tears. Noah sat back down and watched his mother closely as she wiped tears from her face and continued eating. Noah finished eating as silence covered the kitchen area for nearly five minutes.

"Check on her the rest of the night Noah," Pamela instructed through an emotionally cracking voice.

"I'm on it mah…or maybe, you should ask her to move back home?"

"I would love for her to move back, but -"

"Mah that was a long time ago… It's all forgiven, she was young and hard headed, it was a mistake, and plus that chump boyfriend Don`dre is partly-"

"That's enough about it… Don't denounce his character…they both were wrong for what happened...or didn't happen."

Noah stopped his chatter noticing the attitude in his mothers' tone. He finished his plate quietly and took it toward the sink.

"I know she would come home in a blink," uttered Noah facing the wall away from the kitchen table.

"Of course, because you know everything, Mr. Noah`it`all."

Noah giggled and smiled at his mother looking over his shoulder.

"Ahhh, I see what you did there…jokey jokes mah. I do know this though…there's been a bunch of people turning up missing in Philly, men and women, and nobody seems to be getting answers."

"Yeah, right…be certain to check on your sister throughout the night," instructed Pamela. "She needs you."

Noah rinsed his plate and cleaned it with dish soap as he glanced over at his mother.

"She needs me?" Noah objected looking at his mother.

Pamela glanced at Noah and stood from the table and walked through the hallway into the living room area. Noah looked over his shoulder and sat at his mothers' seat and finished her plate of meatloaf and vegetables.

...

Noah strolled quietly across the hall in his socks and ball shorts and tapped on the bedroom door to Melody`s old room. He pushed the door open and walked in. Melody was lying across her old twin bed in pajamas with her cell phone in her hands.

"I saw the light on…you good?"

"Hell no I aint good bro."

"Sorry sis, this whole situation is crazy as hell."

"I know, and I feel so damned useless…my friend is missing and I can't do anything to help…what if she somewhere trapped, or tied up in some perv basement."

"Don't think about it that way, maybe she just left like those cops said."

"Bullshit Noah. Fi aint runaway. Why would she do that?"

Noah sat on the side of the bed and shrugged his shoulders. He pulled a rolled blunt out of his ball shorts.

"You need to chill sis…I got that fire."

Melody sat up on the bed and took the blunt from Noah.

"Why the hell is the entire blunt wet already? Big ass lips man, damn."

"Shut up carton head, meet me in the yard in five minutes, I gotta put a shirt on all this muscular goodness."

Noah shoved Melody and strolled out the room.

"Skinny big lipped runt," Melody said teasing.

• • •

Melody and Noah sat on their back steps in the yard next to each other. Melody took a long pull on the blunt and passed it to Noah as she exhaled.

"Not bad...but definitely not fire."

"You still smokin`it though I see," Noah said placing the blunt to his mouth.

"You got snacks in your room?"

Noah laughed lightly as he exhaled smoke and passed the blunt back.

"You know it...honey buns, grape soda in the freezer, barbecue chips, sunflower seeds."

"Good, I'm gonna need all that."

Melody pulled hard on the blunt and lifted her head to the dark sky and exhaled slowly.

"You need to cut this grass man...weeds and shit everywhere."

Noah looked at Melody and then at the over growth in the yard area. He waived his hand at the needed yard work.

"Garden, smar`den...grass, pass...this right here is my` kinda weed."

Melody and Noah shared a laugh as Noah held up the blunt.

"You know mah want you to come back home right...just for a while."

"Oh yeah," Melody responded inquiringly while looking over at Noah.

"She said so earlier at dinner after you went upstairs."

Melody smiled at her brother.

"All your lies come out so sparkling and silky...you should be a defense lawyer."

Noah laughed. Melody smirked with guarantee.

"Ai`ight...I said it sis, but mah does want you to come home though."

"She aint over it, that whole fucked drama with Don`dre...personally, I aint over it either."

Noah looked at Melody with an empathetic eye.

"His bitch ass still call every once in a while wit'the, "*I was just checkin`on you Pam,*" Bullshit.

"I know mommy still talks to him, she aint over him, or what happened."

"Fuck him, and all that drama, I say why should he be chilling and our family is broken apart…You should come home for a while, we need to mend some family stuff, and until this missing shit blow over…you need to be around family. I got your back Mel."

"I`ll think on it. It's a lot to consider though. I can't just leave my girl Vicky out here on her own…especially since I lost… Fi."

Melody lowered her head at her last statement and Noah noticed her countenance.

"Fiona is coming back…and Victoria…bring her with you, she can share my room."

Melody chuckled and shoved Noah on his shoulder.

"Vicky got that wiz`erk, she can definitely get it," gloated Noah.

"Too young bro."

"Shiiiid, I'm nineteen in three months, Victoria needs me."

Melody giggled and passed Noah the blunt.

"Seriously though…this missing shit got me shook. We gotta deal with too much. Cops shooting us in the streets, niggahs `spraying each other… young Flip got lit up last weekend…dead as shit, seventeen, and now, people just vanishing…black people are being exterminated and nobody paying attention."

"That's horrible about Flip…dudes gotta get off them corners man…You always get deep when you smoke."

"Sis, I'm deep when I'm not getting high, I joke around but, I'm definitely woke though…and the corners, sometimes, it's all a brotha got out here."

"No corners for you though, right?"

"I grab my weed and sell to certain people…my job at the warehouse holding me down for now though…I'm about to join the marines or some shit though. Aint nothing out here in these streets for` real, for `real."

"The Marines? You gotta take a pee test bro," Melody said speculating.

Noah laughed softly.

"Right…gotta clean out first…and I don't smoke all the time."

"My crazy little brother try`na grow up…not the marines though bro, Trump mess around and have you overseas in Cap`a`niggahstan or some shit dodging bullets and shooting other brown people."

Noah smiled and nodded as he looked his sister up and down. Melody smiled.

"Straight facts sis…You gotta come home though Mel."

...

"A heavy knock echoed through the front door and reverberated off the living room walls.

Noah stood up from the sofa and walked to open the door. Melody was seated still wearing her pajamas and head wrap in a chair across from her mother Pamela. Melody never looked up and was constantly texting on her cell phone. Noah looked through the peephole and opened the door as Pamela stood up and Melody put her phone down on the end table.

"Five`O is here mah," Noah avowed as he stood in the doorway.

"Come right in," Pamela said welcoming as she gazed at Noah with side eye.

Two detectives stepped into the living room and showed their identification.

"I`m detective Simmons," the burly white gentleman stated.

"My name is detective Burton Moats," added the slender brother.

"Have a seat gentleman. This is my daughter Melody, I`m Pamela, and that's my son Noah with the bad manners."

Noah closed the door behind the officers and everyone sat down.

"No offense taken Pamela, we hear that, 'Five O' all the time."

"It's actually a hood compliment," stated Moats. "We get called worse."

"Sorry to hear about your friend being missing Melody."

Melody sat forward in the chair and smiled a half smile at Simmons as Moats pulled a note pad and pen from his jacket pocket.

"We`re gonna ask you a few questions about what you remember from seeing Fiona last."

"Okay."

Melody's' cell phone rang and vibrated and she picked it up. She turned it off quickly.

"Sorry."

"When was the last time you saw Fiona Gilliam," asked Simmons.

"She hugged me and walked out of our apartment; my other girlfriend Vicky saw her last…getting in her truck."

"We talked with Victoria Jeffries, she said you guys were clubbing, drinking a bit, had breakfast and went straight home after?"

"Yes, that's right…we had fun. We did all the time."

"At the club, were there any problems, confrontations with anyone?"

"No, it was cool, no problems at all."

"What about after the partying?" Moats proposed.

Melody sat for a second gathering her thoughts.

"No, it was a couple guys' try'na holla, nothing threatening though, just boys being dogs."

"And breakfast went smoothly?" asked Moats.

"Yes. We ate, hash browns, waffles, eggs…drove home and Fi left…she was sober because it was her turn to drive… that's why we went home first. Her car was left outside our apartment though."

"Right. We found her things at the scene…Vicky stated she saw Fiona from the bedroom window about to get into the jeep, did you also see her at the jeep?"

"No, I was in the bathroom already…but Vicky said she was in the truck safe and we went to bed…she was supposed to text us when she got in safe."

"Okay. Around what time was it when Victoria left to go home? And, is there anything else you remember about the night, or something Fiona may have told you about a problem she may have had with a boyfriend, or someone who may have wanted to do her harm?" Simmons asked.

"Fi was dating guys at Temple University, nothing serious though, she left around Five in the morning…everybody loved Fi, she aint have no enemies' as far as I know," Melody explained.

"I have a question," Noah blurted.

"Be quiet son and let the detectives do their job, please," bellowed Pamela.

Noah held his comment.

"Is there any reason you can think of that your friend Fiona might want to purposely disappear?" Moats asked pondering.

"What you mean purposely? Like leave? Nope...not at all."

The room was silent for a few seconds as Moats closed his notepad and glanced around the room.

"You had a question son?"

Noah looked at his mother momentarily and then responded to Simmons.

"I just wanted to ask could this be another situation like the other missing people in the city, and who is looking into missing people?"

"There have been a few missing persons' cases, but each one is different," responded Simmons.

"People are missing, what's different about that?" Noah asked condescendingly.

"Are there any leads on where Fi might be?" Melody interjected.

"Not just yet. What we can tell you all is, this is definitely, a peculiar situation. We found her purse, car keys, and cell phone at the scene...which leads us to believe it wasn't associated with a robbery."

"Hmmm, right, not a stick-up... nobody thinks vanishing people is strange though huh, or somehow connected," ranted Noah sarcastically.

"Enough! Shut your mouth Noah!" chastised Pamela.

Noah exhaled loudly and walked out of the room. Melody looked at the detectives and then over at her mother.

"So now what?" Melody asked.

•••

The 14th police district was winding down on second shift and street officers were trickling in preparing for the third shift. Detectives' Horatio Simmons and Burton Moats were seated at their desks reading statements and typing reports on the crimes they were assigned to in the district.

"I keep hearing that smart mouth kids' voice in my head."

"Over at the Handy house?" responded Moats.

"Yeah. What he asked made a little sense. What if the missing person's cases in the city are connected and we got some kind of serial killer shit going on."

"So, you think we got a serial killer…taking women and men? It's kids missing too, our imaginary killer is grabbing all these people and ain't leaving no bodies…you know, like trophies, ain't that how those psychos' work?"

"It's just a thought to consider. Something is going on and not just here in Philadelphia, but around the entire country. A lot of people are going missing according to the evening news…young women mostly though."

"If so, sooner or later this Philly serial killer gonna slip' up, they all do, and we cuff his psycho ass and bury him under the jail…we just need a shred of something, a tiny bread crumb…so far, it's nothing…that Victoria girl is the first scene where we found a scrap of evidence, the purse, keys and cell."

Simmons took a long swallow of coffee.

"A bit scary man. Whoever is behind this is viciously thorough…nobody sees or hears anything…this joker is definitely some kind of ghost."

"Let's just say, if somebody is grabbing, kidnapping women, and in particular that Victoria Gilliam girl, at around five in the morning, why didn't she scream or yell out? If someone is abducting you and you know your friends are a shout away…why not scream? Or struggle?"

"All good logic and great questions…maybe it's two, three psychos?"

Moats looked up at Simmons and finished typing his report.

"I'm done here…gonna file these reports and head home partner. See you tomorrow," Moats stated as he stood to his feet and stretched.

"See you in the A.M partner…I got a few more lines, I'm gonna pull up locations on the missing persons in the city in the past three months…just fishing for any kind of connection."

"That goofy kid got you over thinking…see you in the morning."

Moats slapped Simmons on his shoulder and strolled out of the desk area of the station and passed a few officers moving about.

...

Moats arrived at his desk the next morning and flopped himself down in his desk chair drinking a large coffee trying to wake himself up completely. He saw a pile of papers stacked in the middle of his desk with a hand written note on top. He wanted to ignore the large pile so he sat quietly sipping his coffee and pulling imaginary lint from his jeans. It was mid-morning and the station was busy with detectives taking phone calls at their desks and street patrol officers moving in and around the open floor.

"Yo Phillips! Who put these papers and files on my desk?"

"That pile was there when I got in here this morning," responded Phillips raising his hands and shrugging his shoulders.

Moats sat his coffee down and grabbed the note and read it. He tossed the note on the desk top and grabbed the first file and opened it. He looked through the report and read it briefly. He looked at a photo of a missing girl, aged nineteen from South Philadelphia. Last seen leaving her part time job at a grocery store where she had worked a weekend shift. He examined the photo of the girl and placed it back in the folder. He opened a second file and there was another missing young woman, aged twenty-six, from Kensington, last seen leaving her job at a movie theater she worked at in Manayunk Roxborough. Moats sat at his desk and looked through the first eight files. After that he shuffled through the remaining printed papers of missing persons. Seventeen missing women from different parts of the city. Eight from the 14th district. All African American women, between the ages of thirteen, and thirty-five. All missing persons, no evidence, no clues, and never heard from or seen since.

Moats sat back in his chair and gazed at the pile of folders and sheets. Simmons strolled in and sat at his desk across from Moats eating a breakfast sandwich and sipping coffee.

"Did you flip through?"

"I did…all of them from our city?"

"All of them from our city, missing in the past five months. I looked deeper and found ten more this past year. Somebody is stealing bodies' partner."

"What are we supposed to do with this? We got one missing, Fiona Gilliam and I think we should work that one case."

"I say we find a connection, something tying these missing women together…at least the ones from our district."

"H...that's the problem, there is nothing connecting them together...no real evidence, no jealous boyfriend, no physical evidence, nothing...just vanishing women...shit, they could be anywhere man."

"That right there is what connects them all...the fact there is no visible, or physical evidence is a connection, that's M.O."

Simmons took a large bite of his sandwich and stared at Moats. Moats rubbed his chin while resting his elbows on his desk.

"Damn." Moats blurted as he opened the top file again and started reading closer.

"Nobody is ever, just missing," Simmons stated with a mouthful of food.

...

4090 Delaware Avenue 10:30 pm

The fenced in parking lot area was filled with cars and ten to twenty mid-sized moving vans. There were vans with license plate tags from Baltimore, New York city, and New Jersey. At the front gates there were men dressed in black coveralls with white armbands holding AR-15 rifles. They wore painters' masks over their faces that filtered out the ash that was drifting downward from the stacks. Around the entire lot, every twenty or thirty feet stood men in pairs with AR-15 rifles and their heads on swivel watching closely.

The vans were parked in rows backed up to the port doors and the port doors were wide open. The lot area was lit up with bright lights beaming from three sides of the building. Four of the seven large electrical generator towers were spewing steam and ash particles from the stacks. The slight breeze that moved through occasionally pushed some of the ash into the Delaware River. The rest of the ash that was cascading down in the lot area like dusty snow was swept and vacuumed. Half a dozen men dressed in black coveralls with blue armbands and painters' masks pushed large brooms through the lot area sweeping piles of debris and ash into piles. Two large motorized vacuum sweeper trucks made zig-zag passes around the lot and sucked the piles into the rear of the vehicles. On the loading docks men moved into, and out of the rear of the vans carrying white body bags inside the plant. The body bags were carefully carried end on end and neatly stacked in sections inside the plant in front of the openings of the electrical bins. Three men teams, stood in front of each of the electrical generators. One man opened the large steel doors and the other two men carried body parts and cadavers to the edge of the concrete and steel entry way. They stacked the bodies three high, in three piles on a large metal trap door that opened and dropped into the floor. They exited the entry way and shut the large steel doors behind them. They peered through small slit in the doors. The doorman pressed a silver button near the door frame and inside the steel floor opened mechanically. The bodies and the parts slid slowly into an open pit of flames. The flames illuminated the inside area and let a blast of heat from the pits. The doorman watched as the other two men carried more body bags toward the opening. After two minutes, the doorman pressed a black knob near the door frame and the intake area depressurized forcing the air in the chamber upward. The heat and smoke escaped upward and the group of men prepared the next pile of bodies. In front of all four of the generators, which had now been converted into oversized crematory furnaces, men emptied the body bags and burned human remains.

...

Archibald Henry III was the director at 'Henry' funeral home. The building sat at the corners of 53rd and Vine streets in the West Philadelphia section of the city. The Henry family business dated back three generations in the mortuary science services business and Archie Henry was continuing the family legacy. He was a sixty something year old African American man with black dyed hair and a small pot belly. The inside of his parlor looked like a museum upon entrance. There were large oil paintings and photos of him and his wife, his parents, and grandparents, hoisted high on the walls. Another section of the parlor had credentials from the Henry family studies and certificates framed and centered for public viewing. Large hand painted vases, four velvet sofas, blue, purple, tan and a full human sized Knight in shining armor finished and filled the carpeted spacing in the parlor. A grieving family sat waiting patiently in the parlor area as soft instrumental music played from a small speaker in the top corner of the ceiling. The waiting family was greeted by Jolene Henry just as a slender brown skinned man strolled in and sat quietly on a sofa across from the family and pulled out his cell phone.

"Thank you for being patient miss Bryant…you and your son can view the body now, come this way," Jolene stated to the family as she glanced over at the brown skinned man in the jogging suit.

Adina Bryant and her son gathered themselves as best they could and started walking slowly behind Jolene. Jolene was short in stature, and a strong business woman who ran the operations at the funeral home. She had wide hips and grey streaks of hair blending in with her natural brown color. They followed her through a doorway draped with heavy velvet curtains and entered into the rear section of the parlor. They strolled reluctantly toward a casket that was under a small shaded spot light in the center of the parlor area. The body of Delvin Bryant was laid out inside dressed in a grey suit. A tall thin man stood next to the casket dressed in a black suit wearing white gloves. Adina stopped a few feet short of the casket and broke down crying as she collapsed to the floor. Her son helped her up and walked her, along with Jolene, back through the velvet doorway to the front parlor area and sat her on the sofa. The brown skinned stranger watched. Adina sat on the sofa crying as her son walked back through the velvet doorway and over to view his brother's body.

"Sorry, your mother is in good hands," Stated the suited man.

He looked through the parlor doorway and escorted Delvin toward the casket with his hand. Delvin walked up and looked at his brother's body in the casket. He fought back his tears and tapped his brothers' stiff chest.

"Do you approve of the work completed," asked the man wearing the black suit.

"Yeah, it's good thanks…my brother looks good," Brandon responded."

"Thank you. We take immense delight in our effort here, and Mr. Henry greatly appreciates your family for entrusting us with your beloved brother…Mr. Henry is in the process of preparing another funeral, and expresses his heartfelt condolences."

"Thanks…do me and my mom need to do anything else here?"

"No sir. We'll see you all at the home going service on Saturday afternoon."

The man wearing the black suit escorted Brandon back out through the velvet curtains and into the parlor where his mother was sipping orange juice and relaxing in the care of Jolene Henry.

"Everything approved," Jolene asked Brandon.

"Yes," responded Brandon. "He looks like himself mom," Brandon added assuring his mother's anxiety.

Adina Bryant smiled and dragged herself to her feet and hugged Brandon tightly. Jolene stood to her feet and escorted the family out the front door exchanging pleasant goodbyes. Jolene strolled past the brown skinned stranger, barely glancing in his direction.

"Tell the boss I'm here, waiting patiently," instructed the brown skin man.

• • •

Archie Henry was in the cellar of the funeral parlor hovered over the body of a deceased African American woman. Archie was wearing a long black smock and a surgical mask covering his face. The females' body on the table was cracked open in the torso area and Archie was stuffing the body cavity with what looked like foam sofa cushioning wrapped in newspaper. Next to the table sat two large cardboard boxes, one filled with newspaper, and the other filled with bundles of shredded foam. A few feet from the table was a cart filled with dozens of shades of make-up and brushes. The stiff body was stretched across a large steel autopsy table. Behind Archie along the wall were four large industrial refrigerators. Along the opposite side of the room were lockers, surgical tool operating supplies, a walk-in refrigeration room and a video screen monitor viewing the upstairs parlor room and front door surroundings. Jolene entered the room and Archie was up to his elbows, stuffing newspaper into the female body on the table.

"Archibald…Urgent phone call…and Demetrius is upstairs in the parlor."

Archie looked up at Jolene and she nodded at him. He moved himself away from the table and over to a small sink. He removed his long black surgical gloves and tossed them into a trash bin. He scrubbed his hands quickly and grabbed a clip board from the wall and made his way to a phone hanging near the doorway entrance.

"This is Archibald Henry…it's going well," he responded to the caller. "I have a moderate supply…over two dozen well preserved kidneys, among other vital organs," Archie confirmed. "Sure, that's fine…I'll be here…and ready."

Archie hung up the phone and flipped a few pages on his clip note board. He looked up at his wife and smiled an unwilling smile.

"They'll be here this evening at 6:30. We should get everything we have ready."

"Okay," Jolene responded customarily.

"I have to close this one and add to the inventory," Archie stated as he passed Jolene the clip board and grabbed a fresh pair of surgical gloves and made his way back to the body on the table. Jolene hung the clipboard back on the wall and looked at her watch checking the time as she strolled out of the room.

"Demetrius," Jolene hissed as she strolled away.

"Go and get ten thousand from the safe, and send him down."

•••

Demetrius strolled into the operating area of the funeral home while Archie Henry was stapling the torso of the woman on the table. Demetrius immediately pulled a handkerchief from his jogging suit jacket pocket and shoved it under his nose as he made his way toward the table where Archie was working. Archie looked up and stopped his work momentarily. He pointed Demetrius to a mask hanging near the lockers. Demetrius walked to the table ignoring Archie's point as Archie removed his gloves.

"You're not supposed to be here until tomorrow."

"Something popped up…I need to take a trip outta'town for a few days, needs my paper today ole'Henry."

"So, I'm functioning according to your going out of town schedule now?"

"It's just a small business favor," Demetrius mumbled through his handkerchief.

Archie grimaced at Demetrius and exhaled loudly.

"Jolene will bring your money in a minute, Archie protested annoyed."

Demetrius smiled and flung his hands out to his sides' palms up. Archie gazed at Demetrius looking him up then down. His large gold chain and gold wristwatch perturbed Archie. Demetrius zipped his jogging suit jacket half way down and struck a flashing pose antagonizing Archie more.

"Life is beautiful ole`Henry…and, how`you stomach this death smell man?"

"You get used to it eventually… Listen, I need you to call before you show up. I don't need you interrupting my business, showing up here, middle of the day, or a potential customer recognizing you from the streets."

Demetrius lowered his handkerchief and gazed at the woman's body on the table and back up at Archie with a scowl.

"Interrupting your bid`ness? Okay ole`Henry…I'm putting bid`ness on your table mutha'fucka…just in case you forgot," Demetrius scolded pointing at the body.

Archie Henry frowned at Demetrius through gripped teeth.

"Right…you need me old man. And I need you. Besides, we work pretty good together…don't we?"

Demetrius leaned over the body on the table and looked at Archie directly in his eyes. Archie remained quiet starring Demetrius down.

"No need to answer ole`man…We`tied together in this thing, I know the answer already…by the way, my price is goin`up."

"Greedy Bastard."

"Don't be that way Henry…I know damn well them people paying you top dollar for the parts…even if they from my dead, used up, heroin addicted hoes like my girl Tammy here."

Demetrius touched the face of the female`s body on the table as he snarled at Archie. Archie reached for a razor-sharp scalpel and Demetrius jumped back, lifted his jacket and flashed his Glock pistol.

"Do not put your hands to my work," Archie groaned fisting the razor-sharp scalpel.

"Take it easy now Henry, dis` just bid`ness…it's not personal. Fifteen thou from now on."

Archie let go of his scalpel and frowned at Demetrius as Jolene strolled into the room eyeing the tension. Jolene walked over and handed her husband a large envelope with the ten thousand inside and started out of the room.

"Be very careful," Jolene hissed threateningly as she cut her eyes at Demetrius.

Demetrius starred at Jolene`s ass admiring the fit on her tan pants suit as she walked away with an attitude.

"Momma Jolene still got it ole`Henry…feisty and spicy! She might need some of this young meat…is you hittin`dat right?"

Archie flung the envelope to Demetrius and it hit him in his chest. Just as he caught the package, Demetrius raised it over his head and then struck a football Heisman trophy pose.

"Good pass! Touch down, we` a damn good team," Demetrius snapped tauntingly.

"Get out of my place of business you criminal," Archie Henry insisted angrily. "One day you`ll go too far…and end up here," Archie stated tapping his autopsy table with his scalpel.

"No need ta`get hostile Henry…do I need to count this? I'll holla at you in a few weeks," Demetrius nagged as he strolled away from the hate filled gaze of Archie.

"I got `da hook`up on Viagra if you need some help wit` dat`ass," Demetrius shouted as he exited through the doorway.

...

The Cotton family lived in the next hundred down the street from the Handy`s. Dante 'Lil Flip' Cotton got his nickname when he was seven years old. Some of the older guys in the neighborhood saw him doing back flips on an old mattress that had been discarded for trash. The younger kids in the hood turned it into an after-school entertainment activity. Flip would do ten back flips in a row for money from the older corner boys who would pay him five dollars for the 'Lil flip' gymnastics show…

Melody and Noah strolled through the front gate at Flips` mother's house and up the stairs through the front door. The front windows and the screen door had steam condensation streaming from all the heat inside the house. Noah and Melody entered the house and it was filled with twenty or so people from the neighborhood sitting around in the small living room area on plastic covered furniture, watching a small television and talking softly enduring the temperature in the crowded room. In the dining room area was another group of ten or so seated around the table that was covered with bags of paper plates, take out Styrofoam containers, canned sodas, and bags of store brought dinner rolls and boxed pound cakes. Melody stopped in the living room talking with friends she knew from the neighborhood that she hadn't seen in a while. Noah dapped a few hands as he made his way to the kitchen.

"Hi Miss Rashida."

Rashida Cotton was at the stove frying fish and chicken. All the burners on top of the stove had a different pan with hot oil bubbling. The back door to the kitchen was wide open exposing the screen door with a fan facing outward pulling heat from the kitchen and blowing it outside through a small window. Next to Rashida was her niece Katrina helping her cook and take orders. Both women looked fatigued with sweat covered brows.

"Hey Noah, thanks for coming out to help," Rashida uttered somberly.

"Sorry about Flip mom…no need to thank me, I'm supposed to be here."

"Hey Noah," Katrina said blushing.

Noah moved further into the kitchen and hugged Rashida, and then Katrina.

"I got Mel with me…we gonna buy two platters each. I need two fish jawns, with yams and greens…plus some of that pound cake."

"Thank you so much," Rashida remarked solemnly.

"Thanks a lot, we got a couple heads in front of you, but we getting`it done."

"No rush, take y`all time," Noah responded to Katrina.

Melody made her way toward the kitchen doorway past stares from a couple guys in the dining area who were checking her out physically.

"Here go carton head Mel right here, she think she cute," Noah belted pointing at his sister while watching the guys checking her out.

"Heyyyy Melody Handy," Rashida exclaimed as cheerfully as she could.

> Simultaneously

"My girl Mel…what`s up," Katrina gushed.

"Heyyyy, y`all," Melody declared as she hugged Rashida, and then Katrina.

"I`m sooo sorry for your loss…and I know that sounds crazy because Flip was like our brother, but I -"

"I know what you mean Mel…no need to explain baby` girl."

Rashida swallowed hard, wiped her brow, then rubbed her hands on her soiled apron and looked down at the floor momentarily.

"What you gonna order Mel?" Noah interjected quickly.

"I'd like two platters, one fish, and one chicken."

"You gonna eat all that…where you puttin` it at?" Rashida stated looking Melody up then down as she regrouped her composure.

"I'll save one for tomorrow," Melody confessed in a sympathetic tone.

Noah stuck his hand in his pocket and pulled a roll of money out. Melody surveyed the tension and mood in the kitchen as Noah flashed his roll.

"Should I pay now…how much?"

Katrina pulled a note pad from her apron and took the food order. Rashida turned away from the money reluctantly and faced the stove. Melody stepped backward as Rashida flipped a few pieces of fish and chicken. Noah moved closer to Katrina and stood directly in front of her.

"That's three fish, and one chicken…what sides you want Mel?"

"String beans and yams with both…Y`all got mac and cheese?"

Katrina nodded yes pointing to the oven.

"I Got it…y`all give us about twenty minutes…forty dollars Noah."

Noah flipped his roll over and gave the smiling Katrina a fifty-dollar bill.

"Keep the extra," Noah stated smoothly.

Katrina smiled at Noah. As she took the money from his hand Noah rubbed her hand gently. Katrina blushed as she shoved the fifty-dollar bill into a metal can on the small kitchen end table near the stove. Melody pulled a twenty-dollar bill from her jean pocket and tapped Rashida on her shoulder. She passed the folded twenty to Rashida who took the money with a disinclined smile and dropped it quickly in the can and returned to frying.

"Thank y`all…gone`have a seat now, around twenty minutes, okay?"

"Thank you, Miss Rashida…for always treating me and Noah like your own."

Melody started out of the kitchen doorway before Rashida could respond. Rashida smiled a half smile and turned her back to Noah and Katrina as a tear streamed her cheek. Rashida continued her work on the stove. Katrina smiled at Noah and he licked his lips, ran his fingertips over one of Katrina's braids and nodded. He winked his eye at Katrina as he made his exit from the kitchen doorway.

•••

Melody and Noah strolled toward home carrying their platters in a plastic bag.

"I'm glad you decided to stay a couple day's sis."

"I figured I need to be around for a minute, to chill out for a few."

"Vicky coming over?" Noah asked smiling hard.

"Boy…didn't I just see you mauling Katrina?"

"Kat is my boo…Vicky is wifey material though."

Noah laughed and Melody joined in.

"You swear you a play'ah."

"From the Himalayas'." Noah uttered as he brushed imaginary dirt off his shoulder.

Melody giggled at Noah.

"We gotta go past the Poppie store, somebody ate all my honey 'buns."

Melody giggled shaking her head no.

"Mel, look at these posts on IG about missing girls and sex trafficking."

"All this is so overwhelming bro, we're living in the last days," Melody stated looking at Noah's phone.

"A grey colored van tried to grab somebody down North yesterday…shit crazy…and those detectives think this a joke."

"That's really crazy scary, and so is having to sell dinners to raise money to bury your son."

"Chill sis, the struggle is really real…I'm sure Flip thought he was gonna live forever."

Melody looked over at Noah shaking her head in disagreement.

"I'm sure he did, but now look… Miss Rashida broken hearted, embarrassed, with no insurance to bury her son who was gettin' money all day on that corner, just to buy Jordan's, weed, and clothes…she gotta get a discount burial service from the Landry's because…ugh, we just gotta do better," Melody said looking down at Noah's feet.

"I hear you sis, but, don't be so judgmental…Yo, he got a baby on the way too," Noah replied looking down at his own Air Jordan sevens.

…

Melody was seated comfortably at the kitchen table in her pajamas talking on her cell phone and eating food from her left-over fish platter. Her hair was wrapped in a floral printed scarf and she had tube socks on her feet.

"I miss you too babe…I'm gonna be back home in a few days. I just needed to be around my family for a minute."

The house phone hanging on the wall in the kitchen rang loudly and Melody stood to her feet.

"Hold on, somebody calling the house phone."

Melody strolled toward the house phone still holding her cell in her hand and picked up the receiver.

"Hello."

There was no response on the other end of the receiver.

"Hello," Melody exclaimed louder into the receiver.

The phone disconnected and she hung it up. She walked back to the table and took her seat.

"I'm done answering this phone, twice somebody hung up on me," Melody said into her cell phone.

"I did that already; the caller ID is saying private number…probably one of my brothers' goofy girlfriends…they hear a females voice and hanging up."

Melody sat back at the table and continued eating her food.

"I'm eating fish, yams and string beans." "Yup, I'm definitely stress eating over here…I bet you will help me burn calories, nasty," Melody stated blushing and giggling into her cell phone.

"Cut it out…I'm gonna see you in a day or two, I promise…Okay, I'll text you good night later…okay, bye."

Melody sat her phone down and started on her food again. Noah strolled into the kitchen area with Katrina behind him carrying two more platters in a bag.

"Mah` called and said she working OT at the job, she gonna be home late."

Noah strolled to the refrigerator and grabbed his grape soda.

"Hey Mel," Katrina spoke.

"Hey Kat. Y`all make out okay selling platters?"

"Um hmm," Katrina replied. "More popping tomorrow. The Landry funeral home hooking us up too."

Melody smiled.

"Noah…mom gonna catch the bus alone after midnight?"

"She always do…I meet her at the corner though when she workin` late."

"Ai`ight…let me ask you a question…in private please."

Melody looked at Katrina and Katrina strolled out of the kitchen through the hallway.

"Your girls call the house? Or do they mostly call your cell?"

"My cell, why? Somebody called and hung up on you…the house phone?"

"Three times…at least."

"Nut ass Don`dre calling. He only talk when mah answer the phone. He do that same shit to me, nut…I`ont even answer the house jawn no more cause I know it's him."

"Ugh…I thought that, I just didn't -"

"Yeah, it`s him…nut ass."

Melody stood quiet for a second with a scowl on her face.

"Why is mom working so late?" "It`s too much stuff going on right now."

Noah gazed at his sister with concerned bewilderment anticipating her figuring out the answer to her own question. Melody didn't respond.

"Mel…when you moved out, your income moved out too. Mah just try`na get a lil `extra paper and keep herself busy... she got more bills and a lot on her mind too."

Melody's scowl turned into a full grimace as she exhaled loudly.

"Right."

"Aye, sis…I'm gonna be busy for about two three hours, do- not -disturb," Noah boasted as he exited the kitchen strolling.

"Ugh, oh my god," Melody replied as she made fake vomiting motion and sound.

…

Melody was on the sofa in the living room watching television through tired sleepy eyes. She'd finally began to dose off a bit after the loud hip hop music blasting from her brothers' bedroom had subsided. Melody looked over and checked her cell phone. She sent a text message and a few seconds later got a response message. The quick return ping message made her smile and she sat her phone on the coffee table. The house phone rang again, once, and then stopped. Five seconds passed and it rang again. Melody looked at the caller ID and rolled her eyes. Noah crept slowly down the stairs with Katrina behind him. He walked toward the front door holding Katrina's hand pulling her gently behind him.

"The phone ring code jawn…ring once, hang up call right back," Noah sneered. "He is ass."

"It's so fucking irking man," Melody replied.

"I'm walking Kat to the crib, then I'm headed to the bus stop to get mah."

"Okay, be careful out there. Text me when you get to the bus stop so I can time you and mom."

"Ai'ight."

"Good night Mel."

"See you later Kat."

"If you wanna roll something…in the small safe in the top of my closet…it's open right now."

"Naw…I'm chilling tonight bro…thanks."

Noah and Katrina walked out and Melody locked the front door behind them. She watched from the doorway as Noah and Katrina strolled into the darkness down the block. Melody started back toward the sofa and the house phone rang again. Melody looked at the phone and it stopped after four rings. Melody flopped herself down in the sofa and folded herself up crossing her legs in front of her. She grabbed the remote and the phone rang again. Melody slammed the remote on the coffee table and grabbed the phone from the table and looked at the caller ID. The caller was private. Melody put the phone to her ear and pressed the button answering it.

"Helloooo," Melody belted in a seething tone.

There was no response on the other end.

"Just say something…you coward, we all know it's you," Melody hissed into the phone.

There was a long pause and then a voice responded.

"Let me speak to your mother, please…it's Don`dre."

"I know it's you," Melody snapped… "She aint in from work yet…you wanna leave a message?"

"How you doin Mel?" Don`dre responded after a pause.

"How am I doing," Melody barked. "Why you wanna know how I'm doing…you called for my mother right?"

"I did…I'm just asking because I saw you on the news, sorry about your friend being missing."

"I'm just fine, I'm getting plenty of exercise running back and forth to the house phone…Is that all you want…or do you have a message?"

"Okay Mel, that's all…Okay, tell your mother I called please."

Melody slammed the phone on the connector angrily and flopped into the sofa. She wriggled herself about on the sofa trying to find comfort. Her shoulders tensed and she ground her teeth like she was chewing food. As her temples vibrated, she grabbed her cell phone and started texting.

•••

Noah and Pamela walked through the front door and Melody was seated on the sofa fully dressed with her duffle bag packed and clutching her purse.

"Mel, what's up?"

"I'm waiting on Tariq to pick me up…I'm going home."

"Hello Melody."

"Hi mom."

"You leaving sis? You said you was chilling for a couple more days?"

Pamela moved across the living room and sat her purse on the table next to the phone. She looked at Melody and waited for her response to Noah's questions.

"I just think I should go."

"What happened that fast?"

Melody hesitated and gazed at Noah. Pamela stood watching. Melody grabbed her cell phone and sent another text to Tariq.

"Nothing happened Noah," Melody uttered. "You had a phone call from Don`dre mom," Melody added agitated.

Pamela looked over Melody's countenance. Noah shook his head.

"Don`dre happened huh? Forget him, don't leave sis, stay another night."

"I already made arrangements to leave. Riq is on his way."

"Wow…is this really about to happen?"

"Did Don leave me a message?"

Melody and Noah gazed at Pamela with disappointment and frustration.

"No, he didn't leave a message mom, but he did hang up on me several times before he finally gathered the courage to say something," Melody retorted sarcastically.

"Courage? He wasn't expecting you to answer, I probably guess."

Melody hung her head in disbelief and disgust at Pamela's response. Melody thought back to the day before when her mother was loving, and endearing in her response to the pain of her best friend being missing, the nurturing instincts her mother displayed in cooking her favorite meatloaf, and sharing heartfelt sympathies. This woman, right now, is the woman she didn't recognize, a stranger, cold and hard who chooses to believe her treacherous boyfriend over her own flesh and blood. Noah braced himself for what he could see impending between his mother and sister.

"Mom, really!" Melody shouted. "WHY THE HELL IS HE STILL CALLING LIKE NOTHING EV- !"

"Don't you raise your voice at me!" Pamela screamed interjecting.

"I pay my phone bill!" Pamela added. "Nobody tells me who can call my house!"

"Yoooo, this ain't happening right now!" Noah interjected loudly.

"Oh, so this is just about a phone bill to you huh?" Melody boasted.

Pamela stood her ground defiantly silent.

"Mel, chill, please!" Noah pleaded as he approached Melody.

"It's something seriously wrong with you…your fucking boyfriend seduced me, your teenage daughter, and would've had fucked her!…and you, you still fucking dating…talking to him on the phone like nothing ever happened…and you still blame me…right! He had his hands up my shirt, and was touching me…I wasn't touching him!"

Pamela stood quiet staring at Melody with insolent eyes. Melody waited for a rescuing retort from her mother that never came. Rage and heartache pushed its way up from Melody's stomach and compressed her heart like a vice. Noah stood frozen examining the pain on his sister and his mother's faces.

"Mel…mom, let's work this out in the morning," Noah insisted pleadingly.

"Let her leave if she wants Noah," Pamela cajoled calmly.

Melody looked at her mother with dagger filled eyes. She grabbed her duffle bag from the sofa and gripped her cell phone. Noah rushed her and tried to stop her. Melody shoved Noah and he retreated in his stance.

"Mom! It was not her fault! Tell her!" Noah attested at the top of his voice.

"Don'dre and me both told her to stop flaunting around the house…half dressed…she chose not to listen!"

"That's not her fault!" Noah screamed.

> Simultaneously

"Don'dre and you told me…pathetic! I was being a fucking teenage girl…and FUCK you and Don'dre!"

Pamela hesitated staring at Melody unable to admit her faults.

"Get your evil, disrespectful ass out of my house!" Pamela shouted.

Melody gripped her bag violently by the straps and strained her way toward the door. She rolled her tearing eyes at her mother and shook her head in disbelief.

"I'm outta 'here…sorry Noah," Melody mumbled, breaking emotionally.

"I won't be back. Your mother has lost her fucking mind," Melody inferred softly.

Melody pushed her way past Noah and bolted through the front door.

"Sis... You should wait for Tariq to get you, it's too late for you to be out by yourself."

"Let her leave Noah...she wants to leave, let her go."

Noah slammed the front door behind Melody.

"You are dead wrong mah! Mel aint do shit wrong and you know it! Both of y'all stubborn as hell...this is some stupid ass shit!"

"WATCH YOUR LANGUAGE IN MY HOUSE!"

"Watch my mouth? Your daughter is begging to reach you...she's hurting because you're siding with that nut ass pervert ex-boyfriend over her...she did absolutely nothing wrong, and in your heart, you know it!"

Pamela walked away from Noah and headed into the kitchen.

"You just gonna walk out...mah!"

Noah stood motionless for a few seconds watching his mother enter the kitchen. He moved quickly toward the front door and pulled it open.

"Mel!" Noah shouted as loud as he could in desperation as he darted outside looking for his sister.

...

Melody walked hurriedly down 5th street making sure she kept a watchful eye on her surroundings. She had her box cutter knife tucked in her hand ready, and made sure she stayed on the well-lit side of the street facing the stores. She spoke to Tariq on the phone and told him she would be at the corner of 5th street and Olney Avenue in ten minutes and he should meet her there because it was the exact amount of time it would take her to get to that corner. Melody strolled past the gas station and the bright lighting at the station gave her brief comfort. She quickened her pace and noticed a mid-sized moving van in the distance with the head lights off moving toward her in the opposite oncoming lane. Melody peered nervously at the driver's side window that had heavy tint. Melody slowed momentarily and the van slowed to a halt directly across from her on the opposite side of the street. Melody quickly pushed her arms through her duffle bag straps and lifted it onto her back like a backpack book bag. Her heart started racing and her knees began shaking. Melody looked back at the gas station and saw a car pull in for gas. Her heart started pounding faster and she thought to run toward the car and station for help. Nervous electricity ran through her spine straight to her brain as her best friend Fiona ran through her mind. She looked down 5th street as the van moved a few feet forward at a slow pace and started into a U-turn moving between her and the gas station. Melody bolted as fast as she could toward 5th street and Olney intersection looking over her shoulder at the mid-sized van as it completed the U-turn. Melody ran hard and fast. She was delighted that she had her sneakers on and that they were tied. As she sprinted, she thought of dropping her bag to the ground so she could move faster. She reached the intersection of 5th street and Olney and ran through the red light and looked back to see the van rolling slowly toward the intersection. Melody pulled her phone out her pocket to call Tariq and the phone rang in her hand.

"WHERE ARE YOU!" Melody shouted frantically into the phone.

Melody disconnected the phone gasping for air and looked across Olney and saw Tariq`s car pull to the corner and flash its head lights. Melody sprinted across the street and a passing car slammed on its breaks stopping just a few feet from Melody`s legs. Melody never looked up at traffic as she sprinted forward. Tariq yelled from his car and quickly got out and stood watching. Melody pointed toward the van as she reached Tariq.

"The van is following me!" Melody gasped frantically out of breath.

The screeching car pulled away slowly at stares from Tariq and a frantic Melody.

"Ya` goofy ass to big ta`be running in the street!" The passing driver shouted.

Tariq reached into the car and grabbed his hand gun from the cup holder and held it to his side.

Tariq looked up and down Olney Avenue scoping for eye witnesses just in case he had to let off a few shots. He refocused on the van while trying to figure out what was going on.

"Get in the car, it`s open," Tariq instructed calmly as he quickly chambered a round.

Melody ran around the car and tossed her bag in and jumped into the front passenger seat watching. The mid-sized van pulled to the corner turned its head lights on and made a right turn and drove slowly down Olney Avenue with the right turn signal blinking. Tariq watched closely as the van made the next available right in the next block just past the grocery store. Tariq jumped into his car and pulled away from the corner quickly.

"Did you peep that shit?" Melody exclaimed nervously still catching air.

"Babe, why you leave your mom`s, I was coming to get you," Tariq asked.

Melody remained quiet as Tariq drove speeding down 5th street looking in his rearview mirror occasionally. Melody glanced out the rear window of the car fearfully every couple of yards that the car traveled. Tariq watched Melody trembling and looking over her shoulder repeatedly. He reached over with his free hand and rested it on Melody`s trembling knee.

"Babe…It's all good, we're safe."

"I hate my crazy mother…I'm never going back there."

"What happened now babe…why you always beef 'in wit'cha mom's?"

Melody slid down in the passenger side seat close to Tariq and wrapped his arm around her shoulder as the car sped away down 5th street toward the boulevard and disappeared in traffic. Melody sat forward in the car, turned the radio up, and sat quietly, never responding to Tariq's question.

…

Demetrius drove down Porter Street in his Mercedes Benz with a small moving truck behind him. He pulled across 21st street and parked near the corner as the truck pulled into the driveway alongside his walk way that led to the front door. The house on the corner was the only one that was detached with a driveway and fenced in rear yard. Demetrius exited his car and waited for the two men in the truck to unload the rear. They started toward the house pulling large boxes on hand trucks and rolled them inside the house.

"Take that straight into the basement, hard right, just through the dining area. Doorway right there," instructed Demetrius.

"Gotta grab them tables from the truck, be right back," responded one of the men.

Demetrius looked around inside his house inspecting the area.

"Missy!"

Demetrius shouted upward at the ceiling. He heard a door open, then shut upstairs and the movement of feet strolling quickly through the hallway. A brown skinned thick framed woman appeared on the stairs dressed in a short robe.

"Hey D, I thought you was comin' back tomorrow?"

"I'm back early…you collect that money from them bitches?"

Missy made her way toward Demetrius and kissed his face twice as she wrapped her arms around his waist. The two men walked through the door carrying two long boxes stacked a top each other. Missy froze and looked as the men entered. Demetrius moved missy away from him dismissing her with his arms. He gazed at Missy.

"It's upstairs," responded Missy humbly.

"Go put clothes on, and put makeup on that shiner," Demetrius instructed.

Missy fingered her messy hair and wiped her left eye that had a dark burgundy bruise around it from a punch she'd received from Demetrius last week. She started back up the stairs carefully holding the bottom of her short robe as the two men made their way through the living room toward the basement.

"You been shopping daddy?" Missy asked trying to alleviate tension.

Demetrius looked at Missy and pointed upward. Missy kept moving and didn't say anything else. She disappeared at the top of the stairs.

"And bring 'dat paper down so I can count it!" Demetrius shouted.

The two men walked back into the living room. Demetrius reached into his pocket and pulled out a large roll of money and peeled away large bills. He gave each driver payment.

"That's everything right?"

"That's all of it."

The two men walked to the door with Demetrius behind them. They exited and Demetrius locked the door. Missy walked down the stairs a few moments later with her face covered with foundation covering her black eye. She had on jeans and a t-shirt, and her hair was combed. She handed Demetrius a bundle of money and he walked into the dining area and through the money on the table.

"It's clean in here...I like that."

"I heard you last time daddy. No more clutter."

"Is that counted right?"

Missy hesitated in her response.

"Who was short?" Demetrius asked scowling.

"Tika was, she said -"

"Bitch I'ont need 'ta hear what she said, it's always some bullshit! How short?"

"Um...I'm sorry D...I don't-"

"Where the fuck they at! Was she high when she came back...short?"

"Yes, she was...they at the trap in Frankford," Missy responded fretfully.

"What- the –fuck- you think'dat means? She come back from trickin`, high, and short on money...what'dat mean Missy?!"

Missy hung her head and didn't respond.

"Call them and tell'um I'll be there in half `an hour, and the money better be straight."

Missy pulled her cell phone out and started her call as Demetrius started counting the money from the table. He counted the bills quickly and then separated them by denomination into piles on the table. He gazed at Missy as the call ended.

"This shit is super light…this aint making no sense."

Missy looked at Demetrius terrified.

"A couple of the other girls came short too," Missy stated softly.

"What the fuck you mean? When I asked you who came short you said one name!"

"I'm sorry daddy, I didn't want to get you angry," Missy said timidly.

Demetrius jumped up from the table and slapped Missy in her face. Missy dropped to the floor like her legs had lost their bones and covered her stinging jaw with her hands.

"You aint doing your job! I can't leave you in charge for one day? You supposed to have my back!"

Missy stayed on the floor looking up at Demetrius as blood trickled from the corner of her mouth and swelling formed under her eye.

"Get the hell outta my face, before I stomp your ass," Demetrius exclaimed angrily.

Missy got off the floor and made her way up the stairs holding her face and checking her bloody lip.

•••

Tika, India, Shine and Mini were in the kitchen collectively making a late breakfast and setting food about the table in the dining area. All of the women were freshly showered and in robes. Tika was a dark-skinned woman around thirty years of age or so. Her head was covered in a wig that had a bob cut in front and she smiled a crooked smile because she tried to hide her missing teeth on the right side. India was a young Spanish woman with dark brown hair and light skin. Demetrius gave her the name India because he said she looked like "one of them bitches with the red dot." India had healing needle marks covering her arms where the veins were damaged and broken. Shine was a skinny, flat breasted white woman with dirty brown hair and tattoo's on her neck and arms. At close examination, you could see needle marks hidden beneath the ink of her tattoo's. Mini was short and chubby. Her hair was dark brown, matching her skin and her butt was so big that it hung over the sides of the chair she was seated in. The women set the table neatly with cheese eggs, bacon, toast, waffles and juice. Each one did a specific thing. They prepared six plates and the chair at the head of the table was where Demetrius sat.

"Who gone`go wake him up?" Tika asked.

"Mini, go wake him please…I was short yesterday, and I aint ready for it."

"I was short last night too," Shine said responding to Tika`s statement.

"Y`all bitches goofy. D aint fuckin `roun when it comes to short money, but Y`all keep playing games…he let us get high on weekends most time -"

"Shut the fuck up Mini…like you Neva` came short wit` money."

"Yea, I was short too, but I`ont wait for him to leave on business, like y`all did…I'm short all the time," Mini responded to Shine.

"Err`body was a lil` short yesterday, shit, it was one of them days, that itch just need to be scratched sometimes…I'll go get him up," India replied.

Mini sat a bottle of orange juice on the table and started toward the living room.

"What`n hell was that noise in the basement last night? Anybody hear that banging…or was it just me?"

"I heard it," responded Tika looking at India.

"I was flying last night. I aint hear shit," Shine stated. "I know one thing, I aint about to ask questions, or take my skinny white ass downstairs either."

The women looked around at each other. India made it half way up the stairs and heard the front bedroom door open. She walked back down and into the dining area. She sat and waited with the other girls. The table settings were neat and each place had utensils', napkins a glass filled with water, and another with juice. Demetrius walked down the stairs and into the dining area dressed in pajama pants and a wife beater t-shirt. He still had crust in the corners of his eyes and his hair was un-brushed. He looked around at the women and then at the table. He sat in his regular chair and looked around at the women again.

"It smells good. Thank you for cooking. Let`s eat."

Demetrius started pouring syrup on his waffles and began eating. The table remained quiet for a few and the only sound was utensils hitting plates.

"Where is Missy at?"

"She said she was going to the poppi store to get more juice," Mini responded.

Demetrius looked at the clock on the wall and at three bottles of juice on the table. Two orange and one apple.

"Did you sleep good daddy," Tika asked smiling.

"Good afternoon," said Shine.

"I cooked the bacon crispy just like you like it," India added.

Mini was eating quickly and had a mouth full of food. Demetrius looked around at the women, ignored their questions, and gazed down the table at Mini and smiled a half smile.

"That food good Mini?" Demetrius asked.

Mini smiled and nodded as she continued chewing with her mouth full of food. The women around the table smiled and giggled a little bit.

"The grub is delicious right?" Demetrius asked as he gazed around the table.

The women responded one at a time, nodding and smiling while proudly agreeing that the food was indeed good. After they all agreed and relaxed, Demetrius slammed his glass of orange juice down on the table breaking it. Juice splashed everywhere and the women tensed and paused from eating.

"Y'all bitches like eating good…and staying in my mutha'fuckin house, but y'all wanna bring me short money, and got the fuckin' nerve to be sitting here like angels!"

The women sat still and focused on Demetrius. The fear consumed the room like a dark cloud of dust that rained down and centered itself on the table.

"All this bullshit 'bout ta' stop! To-day!" Demetrius screamed angrily.

No one moved or said a word. Demetrius stood up from the table quickly. Tika, sitting to his right, and India seated to his left, both flinched and ducked out of the way. Demetrius grabbed his plate of food from the table and yanked the table cloth with his opposite hand pulling toward him. All the food and plates remaining on the table slid, crashed, and scattered around the floor.

"You bitches aint gon'have it both ways…bring the money home so we can all eat. Or nobody fuckin eats but me!"

Demetrius walked away from the table slowly. The women sat motionless. Demetrius mugged the back of Mini's head aggressively as he walked past.

"Clean that shit up off my floor…and Tika go to the store and tell Missy to bring her ass back here."

Tika walked toward the living room after Demetrius made his way up the steps. The other women started cleaning food from the floor. Mini grabbed the bacon and waffles and made sandwiches. She placed them on the kitchen stove as the other women cleaned up the mess.

•••

Noah stood over the toilet bowl urinating in pain. His face was balled up as his stream hit the bottom of the bowl.

"Fuuuuccckkk!"

Noah finished his stream and hustled out of the bathroom at a quick pace. He headed down the hall to his room and grabbed his cell phone. He called Katrina and her phone went straight to voicemail. He grabbed his penis gently and started a rocking motion as if that would relive his pain symptoms. He hesitated before he dialed again.

"Damn…pick up the phone," Noah murmured.

He dialed Katrina's phone and it went straight to voicemail again. Noah slammed his phone on the night stand and got dressed as quickly as he could…

•••

The small doctor's office was in the ground floor of an office building. Noah heard from a couple of his friends that he could get free treatment there if he didn't have insurance and they used discretion at the office. Noah entered the office area and a woman was seated at the counter. Noah walked over slowly.

"How can I help you young man?"

Noah looked around the office at the other people waiting and leaned in close to the counter and spoke just above a whisper.

"I really need to see the doctor, for a, personal reason," mumbled Noah.

The woman nodded and passed Noah a clip board questionnaire.

"Fill out everything in detail, listing ALL your symptoms."

"Ai'ight," Noah whispered. He took the clip board to his seat and filled it out quickly. He sat two seats away from the nearest person so no one could see his chart. He hurriedly walked the clipboard back to the counter and handed it to the attendant. The attendant handed Noah a brown paper bag filled with condoms.

"For next time," the attendant whispered loudly.

"Um…Thanks," responded Noah embarrassed.

Noah walked to his chair and slid down in his seat. He shoved his bag of condoms in his pocket quickly as the attendant shouted from the counter.

"Mr. Noah Handy…we need a urine sample from you."

The woman held up a plastic cup inside a bag. Everyone in the waiting room gazed at Noah as he strolled slowly to the counter and took the cup. He dropped his head and walked to the bathroom as the entire waiting room watched.

"Damn," he mumbled to himself.

…

The nurse capped the vile of blood, wiped Noah`s arm with an alcohol swap and quickly placed a Band-Aid on his arm.

"That's it…Stay seated here…the doctor will be in with your results in several minutes."

"Okay, thank you," responded Noah.

The nurse exited and Noah pulled out his cell phone again. He dialed Katrina and she answered the phone.

"Hello…Yooo, what the hell…you burnt me?"

"Hi Noah…I was just about to call you…I'm so sorry, I was with Trey last week and we did oral without protection," Katrina explained.

"Damn, Trey…that niggah fuckin`wit a hundred bitches though."

"I`m sorry Noah, I usually don't do that…I was stressing about my cousin and… I went to the doctor this morning -"

"I`m at the doctor now, did they tell you what it is?"

"I have to wait for my results…I'm so sorry -"

"We need to be more responsible, it's not just your fault, shit its mine too…you gotta stop fucking with Trey though…I'll call you later when I leave here."

Katrina disconnected the phone call with Noah and he shoved his phone in his pocket.

"Damn," Noah murmured as he bounced his head against the office wall softly.

…

The thin man sat behind his large mahogany wood crafted desk on the telephone. His office was elegantly simple, large desk, two chairs in front diagonal from one another, and a black laptop centered in the midpoint area of his desk. The walls of the office were painted off white with nothing hanging except a crucifix surrounded by a golden circle over a wooden plaque with the initials, KOTGC carved into the wood.

"Our efforts are moving along precisely as planned...the cleaning process is ramping up all across the country, and the blacks are especially a GRAND help... they cannot help themselves...they're shooting one another faster than we can arrest, capture or harvest them," the thin man spoke jovially into the phone receiver.

The thin man laughed loudly as he continued his conversation.

"Oh yes...That ignorant, orange, spray tan painted son of a bitch has no clue as to what the hell he is doing in the white house, let alone our glorious plans...our people on all levels of government have him jumping through hoops, while responding to him with, yes sir Mr. president, and great job sir, leading him to believe his oblivious ass is in control of things, what is a great help...he was born an ignorant racist, yet still...a complete damned fool."

The thin man laughed again hardily.

"Absolutely brother...Our people will reign supreme once again...in a way that our forefathers, who started the cause in 1867 could never have dreamed. We are headed for world domination...Indeed brother; indeed... we`ee are on schedule to release a biological microorganism at the close of the year. We have the vaccine already, all the financial funding we need, and our visual propaganda is on all the major television networks," the thin man continued. "Absolutely, not only are we running the ads for individuals to sign up for bone marrow donations...we also are promoting blood donation through the red cross, while we're collecting all the participants information through our network connections."

"It`s all genius," the thin man concurred as he responded to the caller." "Be certain to remind our people of their needed preparations as we move into that next phase...thank you, I certainly will...power to the Golden Circle, forever."

The thin man placed his phone on the base and reached into his desk and pulled out a cigar, snipped the end and lit it with platinum lighter.

∙∙∙

The doctor knocked and entered the room with a smile. He shook Noah's hand.

"Mr. Handy...I'm doctor Cooper."

"Hello doctor."

"Okay, I've got good news, and bad news...which one do you want first?"

Noah exhaled loudly.

"Bad news first."

"You have Gonorrhea and Chlamydia, that's the bad news."

The doctor looked at Noah over his glasses as Noah sunk down in his chair and leaned his head against the wall again.

"Damn…what the` fu-, damn."

"Damn is right young man…you need to wear a condom. It's a dangerous world out there…protect yourself."

"I'm definitely strapping up from now on Doctor."

Doctor Cooper smiled at Noah.

"More bad news…no sex for at least ten to fifteen days…the good news is, what you have is curable and you're going to be just fine…I'm going to give you a shot, and a supply of pills you need to take with food for seven days, morning and night…got it?"

"Okay, I got it," responded Noah.

"Alright…drop your pants and turn around."

The doctor prepared a needle and filled it with a clear liquid from a small vile bottle he took from a locked cabinet. He shoved the needle into Noah's buttocks and injected him. He cleaned the area and tossed the needle into a hazardous container.

"All done my friend…pick up your pills at the desk. I don't want to see you here for this again…there are condoms at the counter. you should take a handful."

Noah patted his pocket where he shoved the bag of condoms earlier.

"You definitely won't see me again doctor…thank you."

Noah exited the room and started down the hallway. The doctor picked up the phone and dialed an outside line.

"Good afternoon…first one for today's list… black male, Noah Handy, age 19 years, 155-44-1550, he has the shot…directly into his blood stream…it should take approximately two years to acclimatize and mutate itself into his cells…yes, of course…the circle, forever."

The doctor hung up the phone and walked to the next room…

Noah stopped at the desk out front and the attendant handed him a paper bag with his medicine.

"Take care of yourself young man…would you like to contribute to our facility?"

The attendant pointed to a large can on top of the front desk. Noah pulled out ten dollars and dropped it in the can.

"Definitely will be taking better care," Noah said confidently as he walked out the office.

・・・

Pennsylvania Department of Transportation.

2904 s 70th Street Phila. Pa.

Carmela, her two-year-old son, Sherry, and Lacora sat in the DMV waiting for Sherry to take her new driver's license photo. Sherry applied lipstick to her lips as her girlfriends examined her hair and entertained themselves on their cell phones. The DMV was filled with nearly fifty people sitting and waiting as patiently as they could. Some people obviously frustrated by the amount of time it was taking to hear their number called, as others directed their anger at the pace of the attendees were taking with each person they called. A loud voice boomed from across the room near the entrance. A slender black man stood in front of the information attendee shouting.

"The first time I was in this line you said I needed a money order for five dollars…now you saying something different," the lean man argued.

"That's not what I told you sir, please read the instruction pamphlet I handed you," the information attendee said calmly.

The lean man strolled away from the front of the line past twenty others waiting and exited the double doors mumbling profanity under his breath. The others in line quietly checked their paper work and money orders.

"Oh my, he was pissed," Sherry said watching.

"We been here since for`evah, I'm about to get pissed," Lacora noted.

"It's always like this no matter when you gotta come here."

"It's some fine ass brotha`s in here at least…look."

Lacora motioned across the seating toward a guy staring at the group of women.

"He been checking you out Carmela," Sherry said smiling.

"He can come help with some pamper, and milk money if he wants."

The women shared a laugh.

"Carmela It didn't take you long when you got yours done," Sherry stated.

"Nope," argued Lacora.

"I'm just glad I finally passed the darn test," Sherry stated happily.

"Yessss, girl, yesss," cosigned Lacora.

"You gonna let me drive your car to the hotel party this weekend?"

"I'ont know about that…you might not be ready yet," Carmela said teasing.

"Girl, I'm way past ready, I took the test in your car, didn't I?"

"Yes, you did, nervous as hell but you did…I'ont know still…we'll see."

"I need to get a new outfit though…y'all know Ali and them gonna be there."

"Lacora, you're obsessed with Ali…he got somebody though," Sherry noted.

"I can't tell by the way he be all on my shit when he see' me."

Sherry's number flashed on the digital clock in front of the crowded rows of seats and she stood to go take her picture when the attendant yelled her number.

"About time," Lacora mumbled as Sherry made her way to the front.

Sherry passed the attendant her information and he instructed her to take a seat after she signed the electronic key pad.

"Sherron Elise Campbell, organ donor," the attendant stated smiling.

"Yes, that's me," Sherry replied smiling back.

"Focus on the tiny light and smile…and thank you for signing the organ donor card," the attendant stated.

Sherry smiled and gazed at the tiny light. The camera flashed and she examined her photo on the screen at the attendants' desk. She approved and was instructed to wait another several moments for her license to print. Sherry made her way back to her seat with a smile and a jiggling dance celebration. The attendant turned to his right and opened a black lap top computer and typed in Sherry's home address, age, height, ethnicity and estimated weight. The lap top chirped seconds later and the attendant shut it quickly and called the next number.

•••

Carmela pulled her car keys from her jeans as the group strolled toward the car.

"Thank you God for my license," Sherry shouted into the sky.

"Lem'me see your picture girl," Carmela asked.

Sherry passed Carmela her license and Lacora moved close to see.

"It's cute," Sherry bragged.

"Yesss, it is cute," Lacora agreed. "Better than mine."

"Why the hell you sign organ donor girl!" Carmela scolded.

"What! What's wrong with that?" asked Sherry nervously.

"That's a no'no girl…they might let you die so they can give your organs to other people if you ever get hurt or something," Lacora lectured.

"Is that for real though? I thought that was just a myth," Sherry questioned.

"I'ont know girl…I would've never signed to be an organ donor," Carmela stated passing Sherry her license back.

"You just turned eighteen, me and Carmela twenty-two, they would love our young sexy ass organs," Lacora said jokingly as she switched her ass extra hard and outlined her figure with her hands.

The women shared a laugh. Carmela tossed Lacora the car keys.

"Is that, really real though…I mean, do you really know if that's true?"

Lacora and Carmela stared at Sherry with blank expressions on their faces.

"I'll just change it next time, I'll do it over and take organ donor off," Sherry clarified. "Now let's go celebrate bitches."

"Where we going?" Lacora asked.

"And I see you gonna let Lacora drive, but I aint ready though?"

"Girl I'm tired…I'm lugging my son around… Let's go get soul food from Country cooking."

"A Saud platter…I'm wit'it," responded Lacora.

"I'm with that, but I can't drive though," Sherry asked antagonistically as she flashed her new license.

"Y'all see it, don't play 'wit Sherry!"

Carmela twisted her face and the women laughed with Sherry. Carmela loaded her son into the car seat as Lacora jumped behind the wheel.

...

Moats and Simmons sat at their desks in the 14th police district. It was business as usual in the detectives' offices with people moving about.

"The girl Melinda Tate was found…I spoke to her mother on the phone earlier. She was at her boyfriend's house… shacking up."

"The Tate girl is a breath of fresh air…we can close her file. When we asked the mother was it normal for her daughter to run off, she looked right at us and said no. A complete waste of time, and man power," Simmons stated.

"If you ask me…I'd bet a third of these missing women, especially these young girls, are somewhere with their boyfriends."

Moats closed the file and walked it to a bin against the wall outside the door of the Captains office.

"Going to the machine, you good?"

"Two packs of chuckles," Simmons shouted as he gazed through another file on his desk. He looked at the photo of Fiona Middleton as he gazed at notes from the scene trying to find a clue. He mouthed the words, "are you with your boyfriend Fiona?"

A woman detective walked over to Simmons desk area and leaned over the top of his partition. Simmons looked up at her and smiled.

"How's it going H?"

"Nell, detective Gaines…It's frustratingly slow moving…no leads anywhere. We did close one. She was with her boyfriend across town for two weeks…angry with her mother."

"Damn, these teen girls, and…it's the boyfriend most times."

"Hey Gaines, what's going on Cap?" asked Moats as he returned to the desk area.

"Closing a homicide in Summerville, over by the rec center on Ardleigh street," Gaines said confidently as she wiped her hands victoriously. "Piece of cake."

"Lucky you," Moats stated as he tossed one pack of candy on the desk.

> Simultaneously.

"I'd give anything for an old-fashioned homicide case," Simmons mumbled.

"How many do you have right now?"

"It's seven from our area, excluding the one we just closed."

"Damn," Gaines responded to Moats. "Y'all should check with detectives from other districts about missing persons?"

Simmons and Moats looked at each other and then at detective Gaines.

"I thought about that, wasn't sure if there were other investigations going."

Gaines moved into the desk area and grabbed several of the files. She opened three of them.

"East Falls…Center City…South West Philly…call the other districts and see if anyone else has info on missing's…be certain to let me know about the specifics you find."

"It won't hurt to try, what do we have to lose?" Simmons commented.

"It could make our load heavier though."

"Let me know if you need help," Gaines said as she walked away.

"Where is the other pack?" asked Simmons.

"You were just complaining about getting your sugar intake under control…one pack partner."

"I don't eat the black one, so now I'm short a piece of candy."

"What you got against the black chuckle…you don't like black?"

Simmons smiled and pointed at Moats.

∙ ∙ ∙

Moats and Simmons sat in a dinner near Broad Street and Wharton. They sat across from detective Vance Johns from the 1st police district on South 24th street. Detective Johns was a forty something year old man with thinning hair and a full goatee. He wore a polo type shirt buttoned all the way to the top and a navy-blue blazer with his badge clipped in the breast pocket. The waitress approached the table holding a pot of coffee. Moats covered his cup with his hand as Johns and Simmons got refills.

"Thank you," Detective Johns said smiling.

The waitress smiled back at him and walked away. Johns looked at her ass and nodded.

"Your type huh?" Moats asked smiling." "She is nice looking."

"Man, she done told me no fifty times already," Johns stated smiling.

"So, what gives on your missing persons here?" asked Simmons.

"Right…hell, I was hoping y'all had something for me on the missing bodies around town. This aint making no sense…no evidence at all with any of the fourteen missing in our district, it's definitely strange."

"Damn, fourteen?"

"Fourteen…and it's just me workin'um…for now."

"Yikes," responded Simmons. "Life aint fair."

"Hell no," Johns said taking a forked bite of his pie. "How many y'all have?"

"Closed one this morning, leaving us seven," Simmons replied.

"Seven, that all?" "Yeah, life aint fair…best apple pie in Philly right here."

Johns put his fork down on the table and answered his cell phone that started vibrating in his pocket. He listened intently for a minute and disconnected his call.

"Got a female at the station right now…says she knows someone responsible for a missing woman."

Simmons and Moats looked at each other and then at Johns. Johns stood up.

"Y'all should tag along…sit in on my interview with this woman."

Simmons and Moats stood up from the table. They tossed money on the table and headed toward the door. Johns waived at the waitress flirtatiously and she smiled and waved back.

"I think she loves me," Johns bragged as the men exited.

• • •

Missy was seated in a police interview room at a table across from Detective Johns. She had on jeans, a light weight jacket and dark shades. Johns had his note pad writing information. Moats and Simmons sat behind him watching and listening closely.

"This jack ass Demetrius Milton give you that eye you're trying to hide?"

Missy pulled the shades off her face slowly and looked up at the detectives unbothered.

"Got slapped last night, for something that wasn't my fault…but that's his thing, it doesn't matter. I'm tired of being his fucking heavy bag though."

"So, Mrs. Melinda, this story you've shared with us today is a bit…strange to say the least. This wouldn't be a revenge story exaggerated, would it?"

Missy smirked.

"Everything I told you is the truth. If you don't believe it, you don't believe it," Missy said grabbing her shades and putting them back on.

"One final question…how many of your friends are still there?"

"Four…for now," Missy divulged.

Simmons interjected. Detective Johns turned and looked.

"Can I ask a question?"

Detective Johns nodded yes.

"You told us about your friend Tammy…you think he might be responsible for other missing women, or is it just your friend?"

"I only know him to be responsible for my friend Tammy… there is someone else though… and I don't know that person."

Moats moved his chair closer and slid to the edge of his seat as Johns scribbled what Missy said on his note pad.

"Another person you said…and then you just said, four, for now…what exactly does that mean?"

Missy swallowed and exhaled slowly. She looked at Moats and lowered her shades before responding calculatingly.

"Um… D aint smart enough to do much on his own, except pimp women…the missing women…I don't know what they do with them, he aint tell me that."

Missy focused harder on Moats. She removed her shades again.

"Don't I know you?"

"I don't think so…where you think you know me from?" Moats responded.

Missy looked Moats up then down. The interview room was motionless and quiet for a second.

"I really don't know what they… he did with Tammy," Missy reiterated.

"There you go using the word they, a plural pronoun, and then changing that to he…meaning Demetrius and he alone," Simmons surmised.

Missy sat quietly staring at the detectives and wriggling in her seat for close to a minute. The detectives knew Missy was withholding information she knew.

"Are you clean? It's heroin, right?" Moats asked shifting the subject.

"It was crack for a few years. D got me needle popping on H…I aint been high in a few days though."

Missy adjusted herself in her chair as the Detectives stared at her. Moats looked her over checking for visible traces of heroin scars. Aside from the black eye Missy always kept herself visually attractive. She folded her arms across her chest and crossed her legs.

"I gotta ask, cause…you sound like, I mean…you are an intelligent woman…"

Missy smirked and rolled her eyes at the insult turned gesture from Moats.

"How in God's name did you end up in a situation…like -"

"God aint got nothing to do with it. And, how does anybody end up anywhere?" Missy countered.

"Well, some of us, -"

"I thought I was in love," Missy fumed quickly. "None of us got it all together, not even y'all."

The room got quiet again for a full half minute following Missy's verbal counter.

"No judgment here at all," Detective Johns commented. "So, we will run a check on Demetrius, and check out the information you-"

"It's up to y'all to believe it, or not…I'm leaving now?" "I gotta catch a train home in two hours."

"Where is home?" asked Simmons inquisitively.

"I'd rather not say…don't want nobody to know where I'm going."

Detective Johns looked down at his notepad.

"Baltimore Maryland…we looked your info up…it's just procedure," Johns stated.

Missy rolled her eyes again.

"Is there a phone number where we can reach you, your personal information is safe with us." added Johns.

Missy held up a cell phone.

"Don't know how long it's gonna be working, it belongs to D."

"That's fine. we'll take that number."

Missy wrote the number on the note pad and looked around at the detectives and stopped on Moats.

"Are we done here," Missy asked. "No more questions?"

"We're done…unless there's something else you want to tell us."

"I've told you more than enough already," Missy affirmed as she stood to her feet.

The detectives and Missy walked out of the interview room and down the hallway toward the exit. Missy walked out the doorway with her duffle bag and purse. She checked her purse and pulled out her train ticket making sure it was still secure. Amtrak, one way, Florida, the ticket read.

…

Moats and Simmons sat in front of a desk top computer. Moats typed in the information that Missy had given in her interview with Detective Johns.

"Why would she go through the trouble of giving us false information, and a crazy made up story…I put that name in three times…no record exists for Demetrius Milton."

"Jealous, addicted, ex-girlfriend… hell bent on revenge maybe."

"It just doesn't make sense. That story was too elaborate. With the dead girlfriend Tammy and everything. Who does that, with a straight, sincere face?"

"She said he was arrested for assault on another girl last year, he has to be in the system," responded Moats.

"Did she make that up too?"

"Crazy…this entire thing is crazy H…missing bodies, crazy addicts and pimps…sounds like an episode of Jerry Springer meets twilight zone."

Simmons sat back in his chair with a look of frustration on his face. Moats stood up and started to walk away. Simmons pulled out his cell phone.

"Detective Johns…Simmons here…did you run that name the girl Melinda gave you?"

Simmons paused with his ear to the phone.

"Melton, not Milton…got it, thanks."

Simmons disconnected his phone and quickly re-typed the name Demetrius Melton. A photo and arrest history popped on the screen. Drug arrests, assault, possession of an illegal firearm, and pimping and pandering.

"Got it partner," Simmons shouted. "It was Melton instead of Milton, we all heard it wrong…guess it was the Baltimore accent."

Moats walked back over to the desk.

"Well now, look at Mr. Melton…career criminal…do we follow up on the girl Melinda's story, that is the million-dollar question."

"Might as well see how it plays out," Simmons replied. "Play the hand."

•••

Sherry finished curling her hair and applied final coating of lip gloss. She shut her room door and walked down stairs. Her mother was in the living room seated on the sofa watching television. She was already in her bed clothes and a robe.

"I look okay mom?"

"You look nice. What time are you coming in tonight?"

"Um, the party probably gonna be over around 1:30…I'll be home right after."

"And what club is it again?"

"Momma," Sherry responded slightly agitated. "We already talked about this, it's at club Studio 21, on Erie avenue…yes I'm going to be careful, and no, I'm not going to drink."

"Alright Sherry…I'm just making sure I have the information right…you got everything, cell phone, money and stuff?"

"I'm good mom…see you later okay?"

Sherry kissed her mother Althea quickly and hustled out the door before her mother started asking more questions. Althea stood up from the sofa and stepped to the doorway behind Sherry.

"Is Carmela here already?" Shouted Althea.

Sherry shouted yes as she walked to the car. Carmela exited leaving the driver's side door open. Sherry jumped in the driver's seat with a huge smile on her face. Carmela leaned over and honked the horn. Sherry pulled away slowly down Locust Avenue.

•••

Demetrius sat in his Mercedes parked under the El-train over pass on Kensington Avenue just off Allegheny. He watched closely as cars pulled toward the area where Tika, Mini, Shine and India strolled around trying to pick up tricks. His girls worked the shadows under the overpass while dipping into doorways of store fronts and side alleyways turning tricks for pay. Demetrius slid down in his seat and pulled his cell phone out.

"Bitch…I know you see me calling…bring yo'ass home ASAP."

Demetrius disconnected his call and peered through the darkness at his girls. He dialed his house phone with anticipation of Missy answering the phone. The phone rang five times and he disconnected just before the voice recording started.

"Bitch," Demetrius mumbled angrily to himself as he started his car and pulled away from the curb.

•••

Sherry was behind the wheel of Carmela's car driving. Lacora and Carmela were drinking Hennessey and Cîroc out the bottles while passing them back and forth to each other.

"Y'all bitches aint shit," Sherry exclaimed loudly.

The music volume in the car was blaring and Lacora and Carmela were swaying to the beat.

"You wanted to drive trick…so drive…you can't drink yet though," Carmela explained.

"It's just the pre-game bitch…and slow the fuck down please…we aint late, Lacora shouted as she turned her bottle of Henny skyward taking a large gulp.

"Y'all better save me some…I swear."

"It's five more bottles in the trunk…we definitely getting turnt' tonight."

Sherry looked over at Carmela and nodded as she drove down the expressway toward center city.

...

Sherry pulled into the underground parking lot and the three women exited the car and adjusted themselves fixing their hair and clothes. Carmela passed Sherry the Henny bottle and Sherry eagerly turned the remaining liquor up and drank it straight down.

"Damn bitch...I know that shit burn, slow sips."

"I'm out here running late in the game 'cause I had to drive," Responded Sherry.

"I'm whirling already," Lacora said wiping her brow.

"Pass me that bottle bitch."

Lacora passed Sherry her bottle of Cîroc as the women opened the trunk. Sherry sipped the Cîroc bottle twice.

"You'bout to get white girl wasted...mixing them liquors."

"That's the plan," Sherry stated as she continued sipping the Cîroc.

Carmela opened the trunk and put the remaining bottles in her and Lacora's bags and started through the parking lot. Lacora swayed a little bit and caught herself.

"Damn bitch...you drunk already," Sherry stated teasing Lacora.

"Y'all know Im'ma light weight with this drinking shit."

"Pull it together bitches, we just getting started," Carmela stated jovially.

"Turn up," Sherry belted as she finished the Cîroc and sat the bottle next to the rear tire of a car, they strolled past.

...

The hotel rooms were joined. Three of them with the connecting doors open in the center with people passing through. The hotel party was filled with nearly eighty people. There were young women dressed in their best party clothes, tight skirts, designer shoes and purses. Young men, tatted on their necks and knuckles, dressed in skinny tight fitted jeans and Jordan's. Red cups filled to the brim, loud music blaring from a portable radio in the corner, and a heavy layer of weed smoke hovering overhead. People were wall to wall drinking, rolling weed, dancing in groups and partying. Lacora, Carmela and Sherry were huddled together in a corner near one of the beds with Ali and several of his friends smoking and drinking. Lacora struggled to keep her eyes open. In between her thirty second cat naps she caught the glimpse of Ali who continuously smiled at her and blew her air kisses. Carmela fought off advances from guys, one after the other while trying to maintain her drunken swag. Sherry was seated looking around at the party goers trying to hold the contents of her stomach down. The Cîroc and Hennessy, mixed with weed had grabbed hold of her and she was spinning. Her face felt like there were hands pulling her cheeks downward toward the floor leaving her head weighted down. Ali pulled Lacora out of her seat and she buckled in his arms.

"Damnnnn...You` ai`ight!"

The group looked on at Lacora and laughed as her legs jellied. A brown skinned guy shouted from across the room.

"Yooooo, she hit!"

Ali guided Lacora back to her seat and sat her down. Carmela moved closer to Lacora and leaned her body against hers holding her upright and swayed to the music. One of Ali`s friends passed Sherry a blunt and she took a long hard pull. Sherry blew out smoke and stood to her feet and started swaying to the music.

"That's my shit!" Sherry belted loudly.

"Turn up then!" Ali shouted.

Ali and his friends focused their attention on Sherry who was lost in a haze of mixed liquors, music and weed. Several of the guys in the group circled Sherry. One of the guys passed her another full cup of green colored liquor. Sherry looked inside the cup, tasted it, and took a long swallow. She raised the cup in celebration and the guys started dancing around her as the partying continued...

•••

Demetrius pulled his Benz to the curb and exited looking down Allegheny avenue. He strolled toward the middle of the block scanning the area for his girls. Shine walked toward him from the doorway of a vacant building and met him in stride.

"Where the rest of the girls at?"

"Mini in the vacant with a trick. India and Tika both got in cars ten minutes ago."

Demetrius looked around the area.

"It's slow tonight?"

"A little, it's not so bad for a week day though."

Shine pulled a roll of money out of her small purse.

"Hold on to that for now... and take a ride with me."

Demetrius smiled at Shine while staring into her eyes. Shine smiled back. Demetrius started toward his car and Shine followed.

"Should I tell Mini I'm leaving?"

"No...come on...hurry up," Demetrius instructed looking over his shoulders. Demetrius jumped in his car and Shine started to get in the back seat.

"Ride up front with me."

Shine smiled and jumped in the front seat. She looked over at Demetrius and smiled as she looked him up then down.

"You hungry baby?"

"I am...can I get Burger king or something?"

"Ai'ight," Demetrius said as he drove off down Allegheny avenue.

• • •

Moats and Simmons sat near the corner of Porter street slouched down in the front seat of their patrol car watching the corner house where Demetrius lived. Simmons passed Moats the binoculars and took a swig of his drink.

"This just might be a waste of our time," Simmons mumbled.

"The B-more girl sounded so sincere. That is, if we can trust a heroin addicted ex-girlfriend with a grievance."

"At the very least, we can bust him on pimping charges...the missing women thing might be a stretch."

"Right...What kind of man pimps out women and gets them hooked on heroin... Scum."

"Exactly...scum, of the worst kind."

"Mercedes pulling into the driveway," Moats mumbled. "Our boy has a woman with him."

"Just one woman?"

"Just one," Responded Moats. "They're headed inside."

•••

Demetrius and Shine walked the driveway toward the house and entered. Demetrius stopped in the living room with an apprehensive Shine looking at him.

"What's going on D…you still upset about Missy?"

"Fuck Missy…im'bout to make you my new queen…you always been stronger than her."

Shine stood frozen in fear as she crumpled her burger king bag tightly in her nervous hand. Demetrius never said anything complementary or sweet to her with those eyes. Demetrius noticed the fear in Shine's countenance. He reached into his pocket and pulled out a bag of heroin.

"Let's celebrate you becoming the new bottom bitch in this house," Demetrius stated.

Shine looked on reluctantly but took the bag from Demetrius as he moved close to her.

"I can't believe this D, it's a bunch of duties…me though?" "Not Mini, or India?"

"I just told you you're better than them…you've always been better than all of them. You make the most money…you are the sexiest, and the smartest."

Demetrius leaned in and kissed Shine on her cheek and neck romantically.

"Go upstairs and get freshened up, so we can party," Demetrius instructed while holding himself.

Shine smiled nervously and headed up the stairs quietly as Demetrius watched her.

"I'll get everything started down here," Demetrius stated.

•••

Carmela was seated in a chair folded over on her knees with her head in her lap. Lacora was stretched across the floor at her feet. The room floors were covered with empty cups, empty liquor bottles, used condoms and blunt tobacco. The party had started to thin out with the majority of the party goers gone, or so high and drunk that they were asleep in sections of the room on the floor or incapacitated. Ali stood against the wall near the door with his arms wrapped around Sherry who was draped around his body barely able to stand under her own power.

"I gotta pee first," Sherry slurred incoherently.

"Ai'ight, hurry up then cause I'm about to bounce."

Sherry wriggled herself away from Ali and slid across the wall toward the hotel door.

"You want me to walk you?"

"I'm good," Sherry slurred as she wobbled out the hotel door into the hallway making a left. Ali smiled and walked to the door.

"Where you going Yo...the bathroom is that way."

Sherry swayed across the hallway and caught herself against the wall as she turned around and headed in the opposite direction that Ali pointed in. As Sherry wobbled by the door Ali laughed.

"You should let me walk you."

Sherry slid down the hall with the wall holding her up. She never responded to Ali. Ali shut the hotel room door and walked toward his friends.

"Yo...let's bounce...she aint doin'nothing...she high as fuck."

Ali's friends stood up and walked slowly out the room and shut the door behind them.

• • •

Archie Henry was in his parlor preparing a body for a funeral. On his table was a young black woman. Archie was stuffing her torso with foam and newsprint paper. His wife Jolene entered the parlor area with a large cup of coffee and grabbed the television remote. She turned the television on as she passed Archie the coffee.

"You need to see this."

Archie looked up at the television screen as it turned on. The morning news was broadcasting a story surrounding a disappearance of a young black woman found dead at a hotel party.

"They found a young woman in a hotel freezer with her kidneys and liver removed."

"Oh my God," Archie responded in astonishment.

"They are really risking exposure doing this type of work," Jolene cautioned.

"There is no need for that...act of desperation. In a hotel, and they left her there in the freezer. My God, my God...no respect."

Jolene turned the television volume down and starred at Archie as he sipped his coffee and then returned to work on the body. After several minutes passed, Jolene interrupted the silence.

"Would we be able to get out...if we wanted? We've made more than enough money at this point."

"Honey; this is the type of organization you can't just walk away from...We would have to shut everything down, leave the state maybe... change our names and start new somewhere else."

Jolene exhaled loudly. She gazed at Archie with bothered eyes.

"No worries dear…we are going to be okay…just fine honey."

Jolene exited the parlor room leaving Archie to his work. As she passed through the velvet curtains the telephone rang. She walked back in and picked up the phone receiver.

"Henry Funeral services…one moment please."

Jolene listened to the voice on the other end and turned to look at Archie as she extended the phone receiver. Archie made his way to the phone.

"Hello…yes…mandatory 8pm at 4090 Delaware avenue…I'll be there."

Archie returned the phone to the wall and turned as he started toward his work station.

Jolene waited for a response from Archie.

"It's a level red mandatory meeting tonight," Archie muttered tensely.

Jolene watched wrenching her hands as Archie paced back and forth near his autopsy table while drinking his coffee.

"We have to find a way to get out Archie."

• • •

Tika, Mini and India stood at the corner near Kensington Avenue and called Demetrius. Mini held the cell phone and looked at Tika and India.

"Did he answer yet?"

"It's ringing now…y'all better find Shine."

"She know the rules. She probably got in a car with somebody," India stated.

"Hello," Mini said into the phone.

>Simultaneously.

"That bitch goofy…I aint taking no ass` whoopin` cause she out of pocket," said Tika.

Mini held up her hand at Tika and stepped away a few paces. She listened to Demetrius on the phone. Mini looked around at passing cars. She ended the call and turned to India and Tika.

"D said he on his way…he gonna be here in an hour."

"Damnnnn…I'm hungry as shit. We gotta wait another hour?"

"We got a whole hour to find Shine," Mini said responding to India.

"I swear…I'm not taking no beating for this dummy…she better be back in ten minutes."

Mini looked at Tika and India, and then up and down the block.

"Check the doorways y'all, I'll check the vacants and alleys."

The women separated and went in different directions calling out to Shine with loud voices.

...

Detective Johns was inside the industrial sized freezer area of the hotel surrounded by several detectives and a crime scene photographer who was taking photos of the scene. The lobby area near the kitchen freezer was filled with police officers, hotel staff and detectives taking statements from the remaining party goers who spent the night in the hotel rooms. Sherry's body was curled up the the corner of the freezer and she was naked from the waist down. A pool of blood had formed and frozen under her left side near her mid-section. Her body was frozen solid and a strange hue of blue surrounded her fingertips and lips. Ice had formed on the edges of her hair and her eyes were wide open starring at nothing. Detective Johns stood still looking around in deep thought trying to make sense of what he was seeing. A uniformed officer interrupted his thought.

"A couple Detectives here."

Detective Johns looked up to see Moats and Simmons walk into the freezer area.

"Damn," Moats mumbled.

Simmons and Johns shook hands.

"This here is a strange one gents. Kidneys and Liver missing, no sign of struggle, just a weird… surgery, in this freezer…nothing but this young woman…frozen solid missing body parts."

"Damn," Moats repeated.

"What in the hell is going on in our city?" Simmons speculated.

"At this point, only God knows," stated Johns.

"Anybody here know this girl," inquired Moats.

"Two of her friends are out there crying their eyes out…a hotel party, a bunch of high and drunk twenty somethings last night, and this fiasco this morning…Sherron Elise Campbell, from the Germantown section… her two friends out there, all young girls…this baby was just getting started living."

"How does this shit happen in a hotel, and who found the body?"

"Apparently the girl is gone missing when her two friends wake up hung over this morning…they search the hotel floor by floor screaming the girls name until someone in the hotel calls security from them yelling, making so much noise in the hallways."

"Security finds the girl here?" asked Simmons.

"A hotel cook comes in, sees the freezer door cracked, finds the girl frozen…dead."

"God Damn," Moats mumbles. "How the hell they cut her organs out with her in that position?"

Johns, Simmons and Moats looked at the body. Sherry was balled up in the fetal position on her left side with her head pressed against the rear wall of the freezer. Her shirt was raised up to her bra line and her jeans were still buttoned and closed in front.

"She doesn't look like she was in a rumble, no struggle or anything…aside from the blood and missing organs, she looks like she was about to take a nap."

Simmons looked around the freezer again. The storage racks were in tact with boxes of frozen foods and vegetables stacked neatly and lining the walls of the freezer.

"It's definitely no sign of struggle in here," Simmons stated confused.

"Let's talk to the girlfriends, and find out what they know."

The three detectives start out of the freezer toward the kitchen area. Carmela and Lacora were seated on a lounge chair physically inconsolable. Two police officers were standing over them.

"We have a few questions for you ladies," Johns stated. "Let's all take a ride to the station," Johns added.

"I'm gonna take a look at the security footage and talk to the cook, I'll meet you over there."

Moats made his way toward the front desk. Carmela and Lacora stood to their feet hungover and in disbelief. Their friend was dead and her body had been mutilated. Carmela and Lacora glanced toward the freezer area.

"We can't just leave her!" Lacora screamed in agony.

Carmela and Lacora broke down crying and needed to be helped out of the hotel…

• • •

The cars pulled into the front gates outside 4090 on Delaware avenue. Five, six at a time they streamed in. Inside the gate's security was armed with their usual Ar-15 rifles and were dressed in black coveralls with white armbands on their right sleeves wrapping their biceps. Archie Henry pulled into the front gates and flashed his ID card. An armed soldier took his Photo, examined it closely and asked to see Archie's band. Archie reached into his glove box and pulled a red armband from the box and held it up. The soldier examined the band. The band read doctor/surgeon inside a golden circle. A soldier on the opposite side of his car shined a flash light on the glove box as Archie reached.

"Put it on sir…park over there. The surgeons' room is to the right tonight once you enter."

The security soldier pointed and waived the next car to come forward. The next car pulled in and slowed to a stop. The soldier looked inside at the man who was showing his ID car.

"Why are you here tonight?" the Soldier asked as he examined the man's blue armband.

"I was told that clean-up was needed in crematory three."

The soldier pressed the call button on his walkie talkie and waited for a response.

"Are we cleaning tonight?"

"Crematory three," the voice responded. "There will be four others."

The soldier acknowledged the call and pointed then waved the next car into the lot.

• • •

The open space inside 4090 filled with close to one hundred people. They segregated themselves by armband color and made their way into cordoned off rooms made with temporary walls. Archie made his way into the section with forty or fifty other doctors and surgeons all wearing red armbands. Everyone talked softly amongst themselves trying to figure out what the emergency meeting was about. A portly white man entered the area wearing a white shirt and tie wearing a black armband.

"Attention everyone," the portly man bellowed.

The room dropped to a whisper quiet and then silence.

"First things first…the circle thanks you all for your dedication and much needed efforts. Without you, our work would not get finalized…we are in the process of making new and necessary changes from within the organization…we are relieving several of our surgeons from obligation…your services will no longer be needed. We will give each individual demoted tonight, a severance payment, of ten thousand dollars…when I call your name please stand…Christoff Goodman, Archibald Henry, Leonard Bryant, Ahto Harambe, Carmen Maldonado, Raj Singh, Aaron W. Eiseman, Saul Goldman, Erwin J. Hoffman, and Emily Horowitz…please stand."

Archie stood to his feet slowly as he looked around the room. The others who heard their names stood to their feet and looked around examining the others who had been singled out. No one said a thing but everyone in the room recognized the surgeons who had their names called were African American, Jewish, and other doctors of color. The portly white man motioned to a security guard in the rear of the room after he finished calling all the names. The partition door opened and several guards entered and lined the front of the room. They stood like a human wall between the portly man and the surgeons.

"Security will escort you out and give you concluding instruction," the portly man advised.

Archie stood frozen in fear afraid to take a step. He looked left, right, and around the room rapidly thinking of how he could make a rapid escape if needed. His heart pounded in his ears and he thought about Jolene alone at home. Sweat broke on his brow and he swallowed hard. He took several steps forward and started slowly out of the aisle he was seated on. The security team moved calmly and strategically toward the exit and flanked the aisle ways.

"So that's it…you use our skills to exploit organs, and we`re just…fired now!"

The portly man scowled at Erwin Hoffman momentarily.

"So that`s it!" screamed Erwin.

Archie shook at the tension that arose suddenly in the space. The remaining white doctors stood to their feet and Archie moved closer to the exit and was stopped in his heavy-footed tracks by a guard.

"Escort Mr. Erwin out the rear door please," implored the portly man.

Two of the security guards approached Erwin swiftly and aggressively. They pushed their way through the chairs and aisle ways. They grabbed Erwin around his arms and shoulders as he struggled trying to free himself.

"Get your damned hands off me!"

The guards wrestled Erwin to the floor and struck him with the butt end of an AR-15. Erwin crumpled flat to the floor unconscious. The guards dragged him through the rear partition by his arms. Archie leaned toward the exit door and the guard shoved him backward. The faces of the other relieved surgeons turned flush with fear and anguish as they looked around at one another. The remaining white surgeons held their collective breathes, some hung their heads, and a few smiled wickedly.

"We just want to leave…please," Archie whispered to the guard.

"Sorry you had to witness that. We are professional here, my sincere apologies. Mr. Hoffman was also out of line…Now, does anyone else who was relieved have a need to express a grievance?" asked the portly man.

The room was deadly quiet after the portly man asked his question. A few seconds passed and Archie shouted with an insinuated plea for kindheartedness.

"We'd just like to leave…please!"

The portly man nodded and the guards led the remaining surgeons out of the room. Archie exhaled as he looked over his shoulder at the rest of the dismissed doctors. A guard closed the door behind them. As they walked slowly, they were escorted to the front of the plant and were forced into seated in chairs and told to wait.

"What's this…we were told we could leave," Archie protested nervously.

"Sit and wait."

Archie looked at the guard and took a seat at the edge of the row in case he had to run. He would rather attempt to run and fight for his life instead of waiting to be slaughtered without struggle. He scanned to his left gazing at the exit and praying in his mind that they would be able to leave. From the rear of the plant other groups of people were being escorted toward the front. There were guards wearing white armbands; who had their weapons taken away; there were several men wearing blue armbands and the remaining doctors already seated wearing the red armbands. They were grouped together in the seats awaiting a fate unknown. What was clear to the group; everyone who was not white was being terminated from within the KOTGC. The circle was cleaning itself of all Jewish, African American, Arab, and Latin people. The group was herded into the front of the plant and surrounded by guards. They sat in terror for nearly ten minutes before the exit door opened and the 'Thin man' entered wearing a shear mask covering and distorting his face. He was followed by two guards in suit jackets and they wore Black armbands with the initials KOTGC encircled in a gold embroidered hoop.

"It is totally necessary that we'eee make these changes…your services will no longer be needed…our organization has no more necessity for your… kind of people…reee'move your bands…you will receive a payment by weeks end at your homes or places of business establishments…take the payment and resume your lives as you see fit…if you object, or share ANY information about the organization, there will be immediate retribution from the hands of the circle…we`eee know who you are, you should always remember that, and we are EVERYWHERE…you are now relieved," the thin man declared.

The thin man walked out of the area with the suited guards following him. He made his way to the rear of the plant and into another sectioned off room. The group stood to its feet collectively with anticipation and yearning to leave as hastily as possible. Archie started toward the exit as he removed his red armband and dropped it to the floor. He walked hurriedly with heavy feet and weak knees toward the exit door as if he was suffocating and on the other side of that exit door was clean, clear, pure oxygen. Archie looked over his shoulder and the group was close behind him discarding their armbands, some bands already being trampled under eager feet stampeding toward the exit. Archie reached the door first as the selected group of surgeons moved closer with looks of fright, anxiety and desperation on their faces. A guard stopped Archie at the door.

"Two more minutes," the guard instructed.

Archie and the entire group stood staring at the blocked exit petrified.

...

The thin man entered the room at the rear of the plant followed by his personal guards. he walked to the front of the group and they stood to their feet and applauded. the room was filled with white men and women, the majority of them wearing white armbands. The thin man waived his hand as the applause stopped.

"Brothers and sisters…now is the'ee time to press headlong with our termination agenda of the filth on this earth…we`eee are the dominate race on the planet and we`eee will REIGN…it is your responsibility as members of societies policing, education, and military forces, to take full advantage of your authority- and- kill- our -enemy!…But…we`eee must be tactful in our actions, no more foul-ups like the one in Charlottesville Virginia…the day will return when we`eee can ornament them from trees again, and poison their bloodline with disease…Officers, Shoot them where they stand when you pull them over for traffic violations; stalk them in your military ranks and encourage them to harm themselves and each other…do all that you can to trick their minds…exterminate and eradicate our enemy…you have the power to execute it…strangle the life from them…arrest them as often as possible, provoke them to agitation so they want to fight, and then SHOOT THEM DOWN, like old weary dogs…NOW IS OUR TIME!... NOW IS OUR DEFINING MOMENT!... the circle is counting on you! Power to the circle, today…tomorrow…and forever!"

The room erupted in applause as the thin man waived his hand and started his exit.

...

Detective Moats parked his car under the shadow of the EL train overpass at Kensington and H street next to the bank off Allegheny. He looked around and put his car in reverse and backed up a few more feet into the darkest shadowing of the bank building. He pulled a can of beer from his cup holder, cracked it open and drank the entire can straight down. He peered into the darkness near Kensington avenue and waited. After several minutes a figure strolled through the intersection. Moats turned his car on and rolled the driver's side window down and stuck his head out. He spotted a prostitute but didn't like what he saw. He through his empty can onto the street into the trashy roadway and the noise captured the attention of the woman. She turned and started toward his car. The woman reached the driver's side of the car and Moats looked her over.

"You back here in the dark handsome…you need some company?"

"No…get away from my car," Moats threatened flashing his badge.

"Have a good night officer," the woman said as she strolled away quickly.

Moats checked his watch, cracked another beer and drank it down in three gulps. He gazed into the darkness and noticed another woman walking slowly through Allegheny and H street. Moats stuck his head out his window and whistled through his teeth. The woman looked up H street into the darkness but didn't see anyone. She took a few more steps across Allegheny and Moats flashed his headlights getting the woman's attention. She stopped and turned toward the car and made her way up the sidewalk. As she got closer, she looked around and walked into the street away from the car.

"You over here hiding incognito…what you want?"

Moats looked the woman over and gave her an up-nod. The woman hesitated and took a step closer to the car and stopped.

"Come on…I'm not gonna hurt you…get in."

The woman strolled slowly toward the car taking her eyes off of Moats momentarily to check her surroundings. She had on dingy jeans and a sports sweat suit jacket with worn down heels. The woman strolled around the car making sure to brush back her hair with her free hand. She jumped into the passenger side of the car clutching her purse tightly.

"What's in your purse…a taser?"

"No…it's mace…Cayenne pepper flavored mace…a bunch of people turning up missing out here…a safety precaution, you know?"

Moats smiled. The woman flashed a half cheek smile so fast it looked like a nervous twitch. She looked Moats over quickly from head to toe. She eyed the beer can and noticed three more cans on the floor near her feet.

"Cayenne flavor, what`s your name…I'm down here a lot…never seen you before?"

"Three questions in ten seconds…you must be the police or something man?"

The woman reached for the door handle. Moats pressed the door locks and lifted his shirt flashing his badge.

"Damn man ... I aint doing nothing, I'm just try`na go home…shit."

"I'm not gonna lock you up, relax …what's your name I asked," Moats prodded with mannish tone.

"My name is Jane…I'm just going home man."

"Bullshit…a pretty black woman named Jane out here tricking on K and A," Moats snickered antagonizing.

"What`s so funny…my name is Jane…and don't call me a trick."

"Okay, since you wanna lie, and talk slick… I'm locking you up…but first, you are gonna give me your best blow job… Jane."

Jane twisted her face in abhorrence as she looked Moats up then down again.

"Come on officer…if you want head, just say that…and I'm got giving you shit if you plan to arrest me …I'm definitely not that kind of user."

Moats gazed at Jane showing no emotion. Jane gazed right back sternly with her lips twisted.

"Choose- man, shit…either one is fine with me. You won't get both though."

Jane pointed to her mouth, and a second later offered up both her wrists pushed together towards Moats face.

"Choose… which," cajoled Jane.

Moats gazed Jane over. Jane waited.

"I`ll take the head."

"Good choice…plus I'm on probation… I aint got time for jail…I had a long day, and I just wanna get home, get high and nod…now, take your dick out."

Jane reached and pulled a condom out of her purse and ripped it open. She put the condom on her lips and tugged at the beltline of Moats. He pulled his zipper down and exposed himself and Jane put her head in his lap and pushed the condom over his penis with her mouth.

"Whoa…okay Jane," Moats uttered as he pushed the back of Jane's head into his crotch and relaxed his head into the headrest.

...

Moats finished and Jane pulled the condom off and threw it into the street. She reached inside her purse and pulled out a small packet of hand wipes and ripped it open. She wiped Moats clean and he adjusted himself and pulled his zipper shut. Jane wiped her hands and then pulled a travel sized bottle of mouth wash out her purse. She rinsed her mouth quickly and spit out the window.

"A sanitary prostitute, I done seen it all, damn…you give good head though."

"You are so harsh… I'm gonna leave now."

"Hey… you're under arrest, for giving good head," Moats said sarcastically laughing.

"Such a fucking charmer," Jane remarked equally as sarcastic. "I like you…kinda."

Moats cracked a smile and Jane let out a sigh of relief with the half smile. She reached into her purse again and pulled out her ID and showed it to Moats.

"Jane Marie Cooper…damn, Jane really is your name," Moats taunted smiling.

"I told you man…I'm MJ out here in these streets though…don't roll up on me yelling Jane…hey Jane with the good head, come'here baby!"

"Okay MJ…I'll be back again next week," responded Moats laughing.

Jane collected herself and got out of the car. Moats reached into his pocket and called Jane to the driver's side window.

"Yo Jane…hey Jane, with the good head…come here baby!"

Jane looked over her shoulder and shook her head. Moats waived her over. He handed Jane a fifty-dollar bill. Jane folded the bill and stuffed it into her pocket.

"Be careful out here MJ," stated Moats sincerely.

"I will…you never told me your name either…Mr. wonderful."

Moats hesitated before he responded.

"I'm Burton…don't tell nobody."

"Burton…okay, that explains why you're uptight," Jane said giggling. "I'll keep that a secret…Burton."

Jane gave Moats an up-nod and started walking down H street and cut the corner onto Allegheny heading toward Kensington. Moats started his car and pulled out of the shadowed parking spot and drove down to the corner and stopped at the traffic light. He watched Jane strolling slowly down Allegheny avenue. Moats noticed a mid-sized moving van cruising down Allegheny with the headlights off that came to a slow roll. The van honked the horn at Jane. Jane looked up at the van and picked up her pace and kept walking with her head down. Moats looked around in the intersection at all the addicts and dealers moving around under the El tracks. He noticed Demetrius's Mercedes pull to the corner and stop. Moats stalled at the light and watched as Mini, Tika, and India hurried up to the car. Mini was talking to Demetrius explaining to him that Shine had been away from the corner and they couldn't find her. Demetrius shouted and gestured to the women that they better go find her. The women strolled off in different directions as Demetrius leaned against his car and waited. The traffic light turned green again and Moats drove through the intersection on Allegheny and made the first right and circled the block. Moats watched as the women returned one by one without Shine and got into the Mercedes. Demetrius pulled away from the corner shouting at the women and Moats followed behind him down Allegheny avenue. Moats followed the Mercedes out to Broad street and Allegheny into the McDonalds' restaurant. The women exited the car and headed toward the front door. Moats pulled across the street and watched. Demetrius shouted from his drivers' side window and Tika turned around and nodded…

The women exited the restaurant several minutes later carrying bags of food and drinks. Tika reached inside one of the bags while holding two sodas and grabbed French fries and shoved them into her mouth. One of the sodas dropped to the ground splattering everywhere. Demetrius stormed out the car and over to Tika. He snatched the bags from her hand as India and Mini watched tensely. Tika stepped rearward nervously and fumbled the remaining soda spilling some of it on herself and the ground. Demetrius screamed at her and punched her in the chest with his free hand. Tika absorbed the blow with a grimace and caught her breath. Mini and India walked hurriedly to the car and jumped in. Tika stood face to face with Demetrius who was shouting at her. Demetrius screamed obscenities at Tika and pointed her to the car. Moats sat watching from across the street. Tika strolled slowly toward the back seat of the car and Demetrius kicked her in her butt and slapped the back of her head nearly knocking her down. Tika stumbled and Demetrius walked slowly to the car.

"Don't get none of that spilled soda on my fuckin`seat!"

Moats drove across the intersection and pulled right up to the side door of the Mercedes just as Demetrius jumped in. Moats slammed on his breaks, hopped out his car, flashed his badge and pulled his gun on Demetrius. Mini screamed and Moats shouted.

"Get the fuck out of the car…police!"

Demetrius gazed at Moats and put his hands up. Moats pulled the car door open and grabbed Demetrius in his collar and pulled him violently to the ground and dragged him a two feet for angry measure.

"What the fuck… I aint do shit man!"

"Shut up…you are under arrest for assault and battery…you have the right to remain silent -"

"Mini…take my car home!" Demetrius shouted interrupting Moats.

Moats rolled Demetrius over on his stomach and cuffed his hands behind his back. India sat in the back seat and Tika stood still. Moats stood Demetrius to his feet and walked him to his car. He shoved Demetrius in the back seat. Mini got behind the wheel of the Mercedes as Moats approached the car and leaned in.

"Y'all need to get away from this asshole! Get your fucking lives together," Moats stated in a chastising tone.

The three women stared at Moats as he strolled back to his car and jumped in. Demetrius shouted from the back seat as loud as he could.

"My stash is in the closet, bail me out in the morning!"

Tika stared at Demetrius with angry and faltered eyes as she gave him a middle finger salute. Demetrius gazed at Tika with distain.

• • •

India, Mini, and Tika sat in the Livingroom at the house. For the duration of their time with Demetrius, he had never been arrested.

"He said his stash was in the closet."

"You should be the one to bail him out…this shit is your fault," India remarked.

"Fuck you bitch. I dropped a damn soda, he over reacted, like always…AND, fuck him, I'm leaving."

"Y`all, we don't have time to bicker…we need to find the money and go to the station," Mini countered ignoring Tika.

"I'm not going nowhere near his fucking money…you get it Mini."

"Y`all get on my nerves," Mini grumbled.

Mini hustled up the stairs as Tika and India waited in the Livingroom. Mini returned several minutes later empty handed.

"Where is the money?" India asked.

"The only thing in his closet was clothes and shoe boxes."

"Did you look in the shoe boxes?" asked Tika.

"No, I aint look in the boxes."

"Mini…look inside the boxes…shake them, the one with the money will feel different."

"You go do it then!" Mini shouted at India.

The women stood silent for a second staring at each other.

"This is our chance…to take that money…y`all should leave with me…I'm definitely not staying, and if I find his stash, I'm gone."

India and Mini gazed at Tika.

"Fuck D y`all. We can split it and just go. No more slaps, punching and tricking," Tika pleaded.

"I aint got nowhere to go."

"We could all go together," India organized in agreeance.

"That's right Indy, now you thinking straight…how much y`all think is in there?"

"D will find us and kill us for sure," responded Mini.

"Mini! This is our only shot…Missy left, Shine is gone…we should go…FUCK HIM!"

"OKAY?"

Mini nodded yes slowly to India and Tika. India hugged Mini around her neck consoling her fear.

"I'm packing my shit…y`all go get the money and pack…hurry up," instructed Tika.

Mini and India started up the stairs first. Tika walked through the dining area toward the basement door and pulled it open. She started down the stairs slowly and the bottom of the steps had a door at the bottom with a padlock on it. Tika skipped back up the stairs and rummaged through the kitchen drawers. She found a hammer and went back down the stairs. Tika started banging on the lock trying to break it open. The loud bangs reverberated in the closed off doorway and up through the upstairs doorway…

"What the fuck is that?" Mini asked India.

India shook one of the boxes and took the sneaker box lid off. The box was filled with rolls of hundreds and fifty's in rubber bands. India and Mini smiled at each other.

"No turning back now."

"How much you think it is?"

"We can count it later…it's ours though, we sold pussy for it," India affirmed.

India passed Mini the shoe box and the women walked toward the rear bedroom to pack.

"What the hell is she banging," India mumbled.

Tika hammered the lock and it broke away from the door. She pushed the door open and stepped onto the dusty basement floor. She looked around trying to find where Demetrius kept his heroin stash. She toppled a few boxes and looked inside the aluminum cap cover for the heat exhaust. Nothing was there. Tika made her way toward the rear of the basement and could see a blue light illuminating from behind a large plastic tarp that stretched across from wall to wall. Tika moved slowly toward the tarp and ripped it open. Inside was a large refrigerator, a black toolshed case, large bottles of chemicals on a storage rack, and a table with a black plastic sheet covering it. Tika squinted her eyes, hesitated, swallowed hard and took a few steps forward. She raised the hammer to the ready position just in case and looked above her head for a light switch to turn on that would brighten the room. She spotted the chain for the overhead light and pulled it. She saw a safe in the corner and she started toward it quickly with the hammer. She bent forward and pounded at the safe with the hammer several times but the safe didn't budge. A few tiny dents. Tika lifted the safe in both arms and slammed it to the floor. The safe still didn't open. She hammered a few more times as hard as she could and nothing. The safe wouldn't open.

"What the hell are you banging," India shouted from the top of the stairs.

"Come on, let's go…we found the money!" Mini shouted.

"I'm looking for the dope!" Tika yelled as she wacked the safe again.

"Forget that…let's go!"

"Fuck," Tika mumbled.

Tika dropped the hammer and turned to walk away. She glanced at the refrigerator and opened it quickly looking through the freezer. Nothing. She pulled open the refrigerated area open and Inside were two jars. Tika jumped rearward in fear. She slammed the refrigerator door and walked nervously toward the table. She wavered and then snatched the black tarp off.

"OH MY GOD!" Tika shrieked. "OH MY GOD!"

Tika ran as fast as she could through the basement and up the stairs where India and Mini were waiting. Tika reached India and Mini screaming hysterically. She told them what was on the table. India screamed help at the top of her lungs. Mini persuaded everyone to shut up and prepare to leave.

"I have to get my shit," Tika mumbled hysterically.

"It's no time for that. We need to go…now!" Mini urged.

"We just gonna leave…Shine?"

"She fuckin`dead," blurted Tika hysterically. "Dead, dead."

India and Mini grabbed their bags and helped the distraught Tika toward the front door. They hurried through the front door leaving it cracked open. They jumped in the Mercedes and drove away. Shine`s body was strapped to the table with her cold lifeless eyes still open staring at nothing on the ceiling. Her breast plate had a long-crooked cut that was stapled shut with her swollen rotting flesh buckling underneath. Her mid-section was open exposing her intestines, ovaries, and one of her kidneys had been removed. Her mid -section was turning abnormal colors from being exposed and her feet and hands were a decaying color blue. Her torso lay in a small pool of blood that had dried up, and her arm was connected to an IV that ran under the table and was connected to a small pump. The pump machine was off and Shine was way beyond dead.

•••

Simmons and Moats sat across from Demetrius in an interview room at the 35th district. Demetrius was cuffed to the center of the table. A dark bruise was forming under his right swollen eye where Moats had abused him on the ride to the station the night before. Demetrius hadn't slept all night.

"Morning, you piece of shit," Moats stated badgering Demetrius.

"Anything you wanna tell us before you get booked."

"I aint telling y`all shit…and my lawyer gonna deal with you," Demetrius denounced to Moats."

"Keep talking slick and you won't make it to see your lawyer," Moats responded.

Demetrius lifted his middle fingers on both hands.

"We're charging you with assault and battery. Tell us if you know anything about a woman named, Tamika Burns…I think you knew her as Tammy."

Demetrius hesitated before he responded. Missy flashed quickly through his mind.

"Never heard of that person before," Demetrius vacillated.

"Bull shit man…we got a statement saying you know about her disappearance."

"A statement from who?" Demetrius asked probing, grinning.

"So, you do know her?" Simmons inquired.

"I`ont know shit…fuck y`all…and my bail money gonna be here in a couple minutes… if it aint here already."

"Nobody came for you…You think you got it all figured out Pimp boy, scumbag."

Demetrius stared at Moats with a smirk on his face. He was certain his girls wouldn't let him down.

"Smile at me one more time," Moats fumed threateningly. "See if I don't punch you so hard in your mouth, you choke on your front teeth."

"Take it easy partner," Simmons uttered.

Demetrius sat still and continued staring at Moats. A knock echoed through the door and detective Gaines entered and motioned to Simmons. Simmons stood and stepped outside the door leaving Moats in the room with Demetrius.

"My bail money has arrived," Demetrius gloated.

"Shut the hell up," Moats responded angrily as he stood to his feet and pointed his finger in the face of Demetrius.

"Aye…don't leave me in` here wit`dis bully," Demetrius pleaded.

Simmons shut the interview room door.

"Just got a call from a crying woman who says her friend is dead in a basement…her body was hacked up, and… you are not gonna believe where."

Simmons looked at Gaines and waited.

"This assholes address," Detective Gaines said pointing. "2130 Porter street."

"No fucken way. We gotta get over there."

"I can finish the interview here with Moats if you want. You can take Rucker with you…I sent Harrison ahead already to shut the area down…I just called the crime unit, they're in route now."

"Good, I'm headed there right away. Pull Moats out and tell him the latest about our scumbag jack`the`ripper," Simmons encouraged. "Moats already wants to pulverize the guy."

"Got it."

Simmons hustled down the hallway and Gaines knocked on the door again and motioned Moats outside.

"Cap Gaines…what's up?"

Gaines looked Moats over.

"You okay…you look like shit."

"Just tired…long nights on these cases," Moats countered quickly.

"Go and get a coffee. I'll wait until you get back…got valuable info on our pimp."

"Keep an eye on that asshole…he thinks he's a can of oil."

Moats walked quickly toward the break room area. He washed his face and returned with a cup of coffee after several minutes. As he approached the interview room, Gaines was inside talking to Demetrius alone.

"Cap, what's going on…where's H?"

Demetrius sat still and was deathly quiet and staring at Gaines.

"We received an anonymous call…Mutilated body of a female in our boys' basement…21st and Porter streets."

"You are shitting me! Got your ass chump," Moats boasted excitedly. "Where's H?"

"You and me are finishing here with him…I sent detective Simmons to the scene with Harrison and Rucker…soon as we book him, we can head over there."

"Let's finish this asshole then," Moats boasted. "Who's the body in your crib pimp boy?"

Demetrius sat lifeless with a look of terror on his face.

"Well, well, pimp boy… aint got nothing slick to say now huh?" Moats badgered.

"I want to talk with a lawyer," Demetrius stated subjugated as he focused on Gaines.

"Anything you want to…reveal, before you get booked?" asked Gaines.

"No…my lawyer... asap…I'm done talking."

"It's a wrap for you," Moats stated smiling a victorious smile.

"Damned right, it's best you keep your mouth shut," Gaines smirked.

Moats gazed at Demetrius who continuously stared at Gaines with a vacant focus.

"Something you want to tell pimp boy, one final chance," asked Moats. "It might help you if you come clean…confess what you did…be a real man…Tamika Tammy Burns, was one of your victims…yes or no?"

Demetrius sank low in his seat and his face dropped all expression.

"Tell us everything you know…about everything," Moats insisted as he slammed the table.

Demetrius never flinched. He sat gazing at captain Gaines. Gaines smirked at Demetrius and looked up at Moats.

"He's done detective, let him call his lawyer," remarked Gaines.

•••

The church was filled to capacity. Every seat full with people elbow to elbow dressed in their best funeral clothes. Michelle Campbell sat next to her ex-husband on the front row as the pastor delivered the final message for Sherry Elise Campbell. Carmela and Lacora sat behind Michelle crying uncontrollably into handkerchiefs. Rows of flowers lined the open casket. Wreaths from family and strangers alike who'd heard of the frozen and mutilated girl through word of mouth and on the local news. At the rear of the sanctuary local news cameras were allowed to set up and film the ceremony. Heads all across the church were hung low, expressing their grief, disbeliefs and sympathies'. Michelle Campbell sat stoic, while quietly staring at Sherry's body in the casket. Her eyes streamed a constant flow of tears that dripped into her lap.

•••

Simmons, Harrison and Rucker where at the Porter street address taking the lead on the investigation. The entire block was tapped off and plain clothed police officers were keeping news reporters and onlookers from the area surrounding the house. Simmons walked through the bedroom where Tika and Mini shared the space. He looked at the closet and saw half of it empty. A few hangers were on the floor. He looked at photos and pocketed one with Shine, Missy, Tika, Mini and India. He made his way down to the basement after checking the other two bedrooms.

Harrison and Rucker were documenting evidence in the basement. Simmons saw the still closed broken lock on the floor with wood splintering attached to the back of it. He walked to the rear of the basement where Harrison was standing looking around.

"This is some bizarro shit Horacio…a body opened up on the table with a kidney missing."

"Yeah, I seen this before...a young woman downtown in a freezer, same thing."

"The coroner is waiting for us to wrap up, stated detective Rucker."

Simmons made his way to the table and pulled the tarp back. He pulled out his photo and looked at it closely, then at Shine on the table. He shoved the photo back in his pocket as Harrison and Rucker watched.

"What you got there?" asked Harrison.

"A photo from upstairs."

Simmons examined the arms of Shine`s body. He saw broken blood vessels where her arms were healing from needle marks.

"No signs of struggle here?"

Simmons looked around the room as Harrison responded.

"Not really…a broken open safe, probably with that hammer nearby…maybe used to break open the basement door as well. We checked the refrigerator, its empty except for that jar of clear liquid inside."

"Prints on the hammer, the jar, or the safe?"

"A couple of partial prints on the safe…smudged prints on the refrigerator door. that's it so far."

"The girl is only missing one kidney, nothing else?" asked Simmons.

"Looks like it. I'm not a physical doctor, as far as I can tell… Maybe our killer is on some cannibal shit like that last psycho who was eating people for dinner."

"Possibly…what`s strange about these crime scenes…there never seems to be anything leaving major clues, peculiar," Simmons expressed.

...

Moats and Gaines were walking through the lobby toward the elevator with Demetrius in handcuffs. A distraught woman escorted by a police officer stopped them as they stood at the elevator.

"Captain Gaines, this woman says she has information on the missing people in the city, and, that her husband is also missing."

Moats and Gaines looked the woman over as the officer walked away. Demetrius gazed at the woman through wide eyes.

"I'm Gretchen Hoffman, my husband is missing…I need help, please."

"Have a seat there in that chair, we'll return shortly," Gaines instructed.

"When did you see your husband last Mrs.," asked Moats.

"He left the house yesterday to attend a meeting. He left me specific instruction to go to the police if he didn't return," Gretchen explained shuddering.

Moats and Gaines studied the countenance of the woman as Demetrius stood still and quiet.

"Take him back to the box, I'll get started with the statement with Mrs. Hoffman…to find out what she knows about the missing's."

Gaines led Gretchen toward the seated area as Moats pressed the elevator button. Moats shoved Demetrius onto the elevator and the door shut behind them.

"Why'd you kill that woman in your house…talk to me, man to man."

Demetrius stood quiet and in heavy thought.

"All of the sudden you can't hear, or speak english," Moats taunted as he yanked on the cuffs.

"What the fuck man," Demetrius writhed in pain. "Nothing matters, now."

Moats got in the face of Demetrius standing nose to nose.

"A real man would just own the shit he's done…but of course, that aint you."

"If you knew, you'd let me leave…and you would leave too," Demetrius mumbled.

"If I knew what…just tell it pimp boy…help yourself."

Demetrius hung his head low averting his eyes away from Moats.

"I'm trying to help you…you have no idea how deep shit is…I got fifty thousand for you…just let me go detective."

"Fifty thousand, to let you go, nah," Moats said laughing lightly. "You are going to prison for murder…and what you did to that girl, you aint never seeing daylight again."

"Please," Demetrius implored. "They are gonna kill me man."

Moats looked at the terror on Demetrius's face.

"Who- is- they…who`s gonna kill you, and why?" Moats inquired.

The elevator doors opened up to the ground floor of the district. Moats led Demetrius back to the lock box staring at him waiting for him to respond.

"Please man, fifty, cash money a year salary for you," Demetrius whispered pleading.

Moats led Demetrius to the box and uncuffed him. He shoved Demetrius back into the box and slammed the door.

• • •

Gaines was seated and listening to Gretchen talk about her husband when Moats knocked and entered the room. Moats sat in the empty chair and listened as Gretchen finished her story.

"The entire thing is centered around…organs, and the domination of the white race. My husband was paid lots and lots of money to instruct, on most occasion's… and perform these surgeries on people…for their organs…-"

"So, you're saying your husband was a part of this, network of doctors, and others that are stealing human body parts and selling them for profit to the highest bidder…a white supremacist organization is running this?" Gaines asked doubtingly.

"Yes…and it`s so much more complicated. My husband didn't tell me everything…he did mention it`s nationwide, and not just here in Philadelphia."

Moats sat astounded by what he was hearing. He examined Gretchen Hoffman`s demeanor noticing her assured delivery. Her definite tone. She was telling the complete truth Moats deduced. Moats looked at captain Gaines' notepad and it was blank.

"How long you think this has been going on…how long has your husband been involved?" Moats asked.

"Please don't make me go through it again…my husband is missing, and I'm certain the group he works for is behind his disappearance…please, please help me."

Moats glanced at the notepad and then at captain Gaines.

"We are gonna do everything we can, but I need to know everything you know about this...white supremacist group that you say has your husband?"

"Are you one hundred percent sure? What's the name of the group...and where are they located?" Moats asked following up.

Gaines snapped a glance at Moats and then back to Gretchen.

"I...I don't know the name...this last meeting was at, 4090 Delaware avenue...I'm certain of that...and Erwin was nervous about going...he said it was, different, out of the norm."

"What exactly is there at 4090? Did your husband tell you that?"

Moats took the note pad and jotted down information. *4090 Delaware, Gretchen Hoffman, white supremacy, missing organs, missing husband?*

"He didn't want me to know everything...but he told me that address. We are wasting valuable time here...he's in danger, I just know it ... he would never stay out overnight."

"We're gonna help you find your husband," Moats affirmed. "Your husband's name is?"

"Erwin J. Hoffman," Gaines stated in sync with Gretchen Hoffman.

> Simultaneously.

"Erwin J. Hoffman," uttered Gretchen fretfully.

•••

The sun went down on the scene and news crews were still reporting as the police still had the area cordoned off. Neighbors were on camera talking about Demetrius, his hooker house and how it was always some kind of drama going on there. Simmons and Moats were standing a few feet away from the other detectives at the Porter street address talking. Gaines was on her phone a few yards away and Harrison and Rucker were loading evidence with crime scene investigators. The coroner's ambulance drove up and parked. Three people exited the van and went inside pushing a stretcher.

"The guy was scared out of his mind H...he offered me fifty large to let him go. Says I have no idea of the shit I'm getting into."

"This whole thing is getting crazier by the minute. Nothing, no evidence in there worth a damn, besides the girl missing a kidney...like the girl at the hotel party. Everything else seemed to be out of place to me in a peculiar way. Did our guy give any explanation about why, or what the hell was going on in his basement?"

"I couldn't get him to talk…he knows a lot more though I think. Also, a woman named Gretchen Hoffman showed up, says her husband is missing and she knows about the missing people around the city."

Simmons gazed at Moats.

"Hoffman?"

"Her husband is a doctor who was doing organ work for a, you ready…a white terror group…maybe this group is behind all this shit."

"Hmm…we need to grill our boy Demetrius, and talk with this Hoffman woman again."

"Gaines gave the woman a ride home…I have her home address if you wanna spin by there…it's late but I'm sure she aint sleeping. She was terrified about her husband."

"Is Demetrius still in the box?"

"He lawyered up, and after this news fiasco going on out here, I'm sure there are a thousand lawyers ready to take his case first thing in the morning. We might have a few hours before he's processed out."

"We need to try and talk to him again about what he knows."

Moats nodded agreeing.

"4090, on Delaware avenue…the Hoffman woman said her husband gave her that address…we should drive by there too."

"4090, that's the old electric warehouse I think…why would he go there?"

"None of this is making straight line sense…I tell you what though, that woman was scared as shit, and so was pimp boy."

"We're getting closer to closing a few of these murders…this one on Demetrius at least, a cold body carved up in his house…he can't beat that… What's the Hoffman woman's address?"

"A Franklin square address…I wrote it down."

Moats reached into his pocket and pulled out the sheet of paper from the notepad. He passed it to Simmons.

"It's a short drive from here," Simmons said reading the address. "We stop there first and then we press Demetrius for more info…someone has to tell us something so we can connect the dots."

Simmons and Moats walked over to Harrison. Gaines strolled over with Rucker.

"Great work here gentlemen…we can make quick work of this one. Our perp can't escape the evidence of a corpse in his house."

"It's definitely a done deal for this joker," stated Harrison.

"We're headed back to the station, see you there," said Simmons.

Moats and Simmons started walking away.

"You know that chick doesn't take interview notes…she memorizes all the details."

"What's that partner?"

"Gaines…she doesn't take notes when she interviews. When she questioned pimp boy, and the Hoffman woman, she never wrote anything down…never filed anything."

"Really…she is thorough…she made captain for a reason I suppose."

…

Simmons drove slowly down north 4th street with Moats riding shotgun. The street was lined with old world styled homes and three storied Victorian homes. The one-way street was lined with cars as they pulled to a stop at the address.

"Nowhere to park," Moats pondered looking around.

"Right…that's the problem with these areas. All this money, and no parking."

Simmons looked up at the front facing room at the address as he stalled the car in front putting it in park in the middle of the street.

"You sure this is it?"

Moats looked at his notes again.

"437 north 4th street…that's it."

"It's completely dark downstairs, and the upstairs front room light just turned off."

"What you think…knock, or wait until the morning?"

"I think we should wait until morning. She's probably trying to finally get rest."

"Your call H…we need more info from her, but we can hit it first thing in the a.m."

Simmons hesitated and reached inside his jacket pocket and pulled out the photo he took from Porter street.

"First thing in the morning partner…what I really want to do, is find these girls."

Simmons handed Moats the photo.

"Took that from the Porter street address. The white girl with the sand color hair was on the table carved up…if we can find and talk to one of the others, we can really get some detailed information…that's our Baltimore girl there in the blue shorts."

"I recognize the Baltimore girl…let's get info straight from the horse's mouth," Moats uttered gazing at the picture.

"I'm one hundred percent certain that, at least two other girls were in that house recently."

"I have an idea where they might be."

"Where is that?"

"These chicks are creatures of habit…and their habit takes them to K and A."

"Kensington and Allegheny, of course, heroin capitol."

Simmons put the car in drive and pulled slowly down 4th street.

"Let's do a drive through to see if we can spot those girls," said Simmons.

"Let's hit it."

As the detective's car drove away down 4th street the front door of 437 opened slowly. Two figures exited slowly pulling the door closed behind them. They were dressed in dark colored jumpsuits, black face coverings and gloves. They both pocketed their pistols as they walked down 4th street and jumped into a white mini van parked on the corner. They started the car and drove away in the same direction as Moats and Simmons.

...

Simmons parked near the bank on H street at the direction of Moats. The car was in the shadows as the two detectives exited and started walking toward the corner slowly. Kensington and Allegheny was bustling with heroin addicts strolling around with no destination, dope dealers in the shadows, and girls working the corners for money and drugs.

"This place is a zoo."

"Tell me about it…if those girls are anywhere, they're out here," stated Moats.

They strolled leisurely toward the corner trying to blend in but it wasn't working. They walked past a couple of dealers who gave them the once over. Moats unholstered his Glock pistol.

"Don't fucking run…turn around," Moats directed at the two thugs pointing his gun.

The two guys turned and faced the wall of the building they were standing in front of. Moats patted them down emptying their pockets of money. He grabbed one of them in the collar and turned him around.

"Y'all seen any of these girls out here tonight…don't fucking lie."

Simmons showed the thug the photo he took from Porter street. The thug barely looked at the photo and shook his head no.

"Don't B.S us now," Simmons advised as Moats shoved the photo closer to the face of the thug.

"I said no."

Moats shoved the thug in the back of his head and placed his right foot on the roll of money that was on the ground. The thug looked down at his earnings for the day and walked quickly away up the street. Moats grabbed the other thug and showed him the picture. Simmons shined a pen light on the photo.

"Look closely," Simmons instructed.

"Don't fuck your money up like your boy just did…you seen any of these girls?"

The thug looked at the picture and down at his bundle of money that Moats had dropped in front of him. The thug glanced at the roll of money under Moats right foot, and then up at Moats.

"If your vision is clear, you can have that bundle of money, plus yours."

The thug gazed at Moats. He pointed at the picture.

"The trick they call Mini just grabbed a bag off me…they needle-pop behind the check cashing jawn."

"You sure," Moats asked.

"I'm sure…That's her…everybody knows short Mini, she` the best, at everything."

Moats picked up the money from under his right foot. He peeled away half and gave it to the thug. He shoved the rest in his pocket. He picked up the other bundle he`d taken from the thugs' pocket and handed it to him. He shoved the thug in his collar forcing him toward the bank.

"Kick rocks…if I catch you slipping out here again, you`re taking the ride."

The thug frowned at Moats as he strolled away slowly. Simmons and Moats crossed the street headed toward the rear of the check cashing store. As they entered the crossing, a loud whistle echoed under the bridge area followed by a booming shouting voice.

"Five oh out here!!! FIVE OH!" shouted the dealer thug.

The thug shouted as loud as he could as he ran into the darkness under the bridge. Simmons looked at Moats and they started trotting toward the rear of the check cashing store on Allegheny. The corners started clearing in different directions as prostitutes, dealers and customers started to disperse. Moats reached the rear of the check cashing store before Simmons who was lagging behind gasping for air. When he reached the rear driveway, Moats walked slowly down the driveway facing the rear of the check cashing store. He pulled out his pen light. Four or five people were there seated on the steps slumped over nodding. Moats approached and looked at two of the black women. The ground was littered with trash, used condoms and disposable needles. He adjusted his head trying to see their faces that were hung low and leaning over. Two of the other women were laying across each other. He gently lifted one of the women's head and shined his pen light. He squinted and shined his pen light closer on the woman's face and the woman moaned and slightly lifted her head

"Get off `agh meee, foe` I peppa spray yo'ass," the woman slurred as a long strand of slobber dripped out of the side of her mouth. It was Jane Marie. Moats lowered her head.

"Damn…MJ," Moats uttered sorrowfully as the image of him holding her identification card flashed in his mind.

Moats looked over his shoulder and Simmons was trotting down the driveway slowly.

"I've gotta lose some weight partner," Simmons mouthed gasping for air and bent over.

"Is this her…I need to see the picture again."

Moats lifted the head of the other woman. Moats shined his pen light and tapped the woman's face gently. His mind flashed back to the McDonald's parking lot but he still wasn't sure.

"Nooooo, Not right now nig'gah damn," Mini slurred and continued nodding.

"That's her," Simmons confirmed pointing at Mini in the photo.

"Mini, yeah, I remember now, the driver…Mini…come on chick, we taking a ride," Moats said as he started lifting Mini from the steps. Simmons leaned in to help.

"What`n`da fuck y`all want?" Mini slurred looking at Moats, then Simmons.

They got Mini to her feet and guided her down the driveway with her swaying and cussing. Moats looked over his shoulder at MJ who was leaning and drooling. She collapsed to the bottom step and curled up.

"Damn man…y`all fuckin`up my flight," Mini reprimanded, slurring her words.

...

Archie Henry was upstairs in his bedroom with Jolene hurriedly packing clothes. A large suitcase was open on the bed and Jolene was frantically moving from her closet and shoving clothing into a large duffle bag on the opposite side of the bed.

"We can't take everything…just the essentials," Archie mumbled nervously.

"What's the plan…where should we go?"

"I'm not sure…we just have to leave here…this city."

"Archie…are we gonna be okay," Jolene asked quivering as she stopped moving.

Archie stared at her with unsure eyes.

"We are going to be fine…keep packing dear wife, we need to go as soon as possible."

"Honey…the two bodies in the parlor?"

Archie stared at Jolene with a despairing unsympathetic compassion.

"No time for that…we need to leave. It's a matter of life and death for us."

Jolene examined the coldness of her husbands' statement. She understood that he would never abandon his profession and his actions were clear conformation that he was afraid of what was looming. Jolene shoved more of her clothing into the duffle bag and zipped it shut. Archie grabbed a couple of suits from his closet and threw them into his suitcase. He moved hurriedly to the bottom of his closet and opened a large safe in the corner. He spun the combination quickly and pulled it open. He started removing stacks of cash and carried it to his suitcase and tossed it in. He emptied nearly two hundred thousand and stuffed it in with his clothing and slammed the suitcase shut. He reached inside the top of his closet and pulled down his revolver and made certain it was loaded. Jolene stopped and watched as Archie checked the gun.

"Don't stand watching me honey…you got everything you need?"

"Nothing else will fit," Jolene stated worrying.

"We can replace the things…they are just things," Archie clarified.

Jolene continued watching.

"I'll take the bags to the car…grab our passports from the safe."

Jolene went toward the safe and Archie carried the duffle bag out of the room and down the stairs.

• • •

Simmons was at his desk waiting for Moats to arrive. He finished off his second breakfast sandwich and took a large gulp of his coffee. Moats walked in wearing the same clothes from the late night before. His eyes were swollen and he was physically drained.

"Did you get any sleep?"

"Maybe an hour…maybe two. I'm grabbing a coffee, then we can talk to the girl Mini, and then Pimp boy."

"I talked to the girl already…Let`s get moving on Demetrius…we still need to drive over to the Hoffman house too."

Moats nodded and left to get his coffee. Captain Gaines made her way to the desk area.

"We are done with Demetrius Melton, his lawyer is on his way now," Gaines reported.

"I'm gonna ask him a few questions about the girl in his house before he's transported."

"Tried that yesterday…he's tight as a clam."

"Maybe I'll be a little gentle with him…see if that works," Simmons said smiling.

"The girl in the box?"

Simmons hesitated.

"We picked her up on prostitution and drug charges last night. She's sleeping one off."

"Okay," Gaines said.

Moats returned with his coffee and drank large gulps. Gaines walked away and Moats stared at her ass.

"I'd try it…maybe once."

"Focus man," Simmons said as he grabbed a breakfast bag from his desk.

He reached inside and pulled out a breakfast sandwich and orange juice. Moats held out his hand and Simmons shook his head no.

"For Demetrius."

"Huh?"

"The soft glove approach… Let me do the talking this time…you scare the bejesus out of Demetrius."

"Okay…your lead…but I could' a used a sausage egg and cheese jawn."

…

Demetrius finished the sandwich and juice Simmons gave him. Moats sat in a chair fuming, quietly staring at Demetrius.

"How you holding up down in the box?"

"That lock-up is the least of my problems right now."

"Alright…I need you to help me out a little. I heard you offered my partner here a stipend for your release…that's not going to happen, but if you give me a little something to go on, I can definitely help you out later when the shit really gets thick for you…body in your basement…prostitutes telling your business… We arrested, Minerva Middleton last night…you call her Mini…she told us a few things about, the family business."

"Mini talking huh?"

Simmons hesitated and flashed Demetrius a smirking face.

"She said she tried to stop the other girl Tika from breaking into your safe…the one in the basement, next to -"

"Tika broke in my safe," Demetrius interjected fuming.

Simmons sat quietly staring at Demetrius. Moats folded his arms and waited.

"Bitches…where the fuck is …can't trust a dirty trick, damn."

"What was in the safe…help us out."

"Man, listen…this shit is colossal…y'all don't know how big."

"Tell us then."

Demetrius hung his head. Simmons waited and Moats inclined. Demetrius looked up at the video recorder and then at Simmons. Moats stood up and left the room. He returned a few seconds later.

"I turned the recorder off," ensured Moats.

"Let's hear it then…give me something," Simmons encouraged.

Demetrius swallowed hard.

"My ass is on the chopping block…this shit is leveled up to the sky…y'all aint ready man…seriously, I'm -"

"Try us Demetrius, we can handle it," Moats interjected.

"All I know is, these people were paying long money… for body parts, don't care where they came from…I was working with a couple funeral directors, Archibald Henry, over on 54th street, and another guy named Conrad Boykins, his place is in Mt. Airy. They paid me big coins to run my girls down on heroin, and turn their bodies over to them…they cut the bodies up for parts, like a car chop shop… and sell them to the highest, white bidder…the game is being run by a group…my getaway money, and my ledger book was in my safe…that book was my only leverage…if Tika, Mini or any of them bitches got that book, they assess are in serious danger. It had names in it, that I heard from time to time from Archie and Conrad…the payments they gave me, down to the dollar…understand this man, these people are running the fucking world man, I'm talking politicians, doctors, military, news networks, and police captains… you hear what I'm saying?"

Simmons and Moats sat still in stunned silence.

"Aint no way out of this shit for me…they know I'm talking, so I'm thru."

"We'll try to help you."

"You aint hear me big man…it's done…I'm done…y'all are fucking done."

"You one hundred percent sure…about our captain?"

Demetrius smiled an overwhelmed sarcastic smile.

"She asked me if my mother and sister still lived in Brewery town…read off my mom's address, and told me to be careful as to what I say."

Simmons turned and looked at Moats. They both gazed at Demetrius processing what they'd just heard.

"Told y'all it was big…make sure my momma and sister are straight man…that's all I need…keep my folks safe…please."

•••

Moats and Simmons exited the police station under watchful eyes of captain Gaines and others. They booked Mini on prostitution charges, walked her down to the ground floor in handcuffs for processing. Instead of booking her, they led her out the side door of the building and told her not to mention her connection to Demetrius to anyone and assured her it was a matter of life and death. They further advised Mini to leave the city, and gave her that message to pass on to her friends Tika and India…

Moats was speeding toward Franklin Square trying to get to Gretchen Hoffman's house. They entered the freeway and Moats punched the gas and placed his red light on top of his car…

They double parked in front of 437 and exited the car surveying the area. They approached the door and Simmons knocked hard. The front door swung open slowly. Moats and Simmons pulled their guns and stepped inside.

"Should we call for back-up?"

"Who can we trust?" Simmons responded.

The detectives swept the ground floor of the house carefully.

"Gretchen Hoffman…POLICE!" Moats shouted.

There was no response. The detectives made their way up the stairs and into the front room where they saw the light shut off the night before. Gretchen was stretched across the bed bleeding and dead. Her throat was slashed on her jugular veins and the sheets resting beneath her head and neck were drenched with blood. She'd bled completely out and was turning blue. Moats put out a call for an ambulance. Simmons made a personal call on his cell to detective Vance Johns from the 1st police district on south 24th street.

"Detective Johns…Simmons, from the 35th…I have a break in these missing body cases…grab a few guys that you trust with your life, and wait for my next call in a few hours."

"This is big, big," Simmons noted to Johns.

Simmons disconnected his call.

"Gaines was with her last…gave her a ride home," Moats explained.

Simmons and Moats stared at each other.

"Demetrius said Gaines is part of it…Gretchen here says her missing husband was working for the group…and bodies are piling up, and going missing all around the city…My God."

"We done stepped in the shit pile now…we are up to our knees in it…might as well start flinging it around," Moats declared.

"Hell yeah," Simmons avowed.

The two detectives looked around for physical clues at the scene.

...

The detectives parked their car on 54th street directly in front of the funeral parlor. They walked past a mid-sized white van parked in the driveway and noticed a Mercedes wagon parked behind it loaded with bags and suitcases. Moats and Simmons walked up the front stairs and pressed the buzzer on the front door. They waited a few seconds and Simmons pushed the front door gently as Moats pressed the buzzer again. The front door opened slowly and swung back closed.

"Damn…another open door," Simmons groaned.

Moats pushed the door open wide, pulled his gun and rushed in with Simmons close behind.

"POLICE!"

The detectives entered and made their way through the velvet curtains toward the casket display area. They looked at the body of a young man dressed in a blue suit lying in the casket. Moats pointed to a door and the detectives walked over. They opened the door and on the other side was Archie's work area. There were two bodies on autopsy tables covered under white sheets. The air conditioning was on high making the room feel like the inside of a refrigerator. The detectives scanned the area with their guns drawn.

"Archibald Henry!" Simmons shouted loudly.

There was no response. They moved further back into the area and saw a black man tied to a chair slouched over with his back to them. The detectives approached slowly. The man was dressed in a black suit and had on white gloves. The chair he was seated in was soaked with his urine and excrement under his buttocks. His throat was slit on his jugular veins and he had bled to death. His white shirt collar was stained red. At his feet was a large scalpel used for surgery during autopsies'. Across the room, the refrigerators' in Archie`s work area were wide open and all the containers where he`d stored his organs were empty. Moats and Simmons searched the entire work area looking for and documenting evidence. They searched the upstairs bedrooms and the front office. Simmons called the scene in over the radio as the detectives exited the funeral home and holstered their weapons.

"The cleanup has begun partner... was that our guy Archibald Henry?"

"They are definitely cleaning house... That's definitely not Archibald, according to that large photo in the parlor area. That's gotta be him and his wife in that picture…that guy was a white glove worker."

"Right…so maybe the Henry`s skipped town," Moats insinuated relived.

Simmons looked inside the Mercedes.

"They were definitely planning on leaving in a hurry. Bodies on the tables, bags packed."

Moats walked to the back of the white work van in the driveway. He wiggled on the door handle and it unlocked in his hand. He stopped and looked at Simmons and shook his head left to right.

"Another open door…hell, we got a shit storm of murders, we aint got nothing to lose."

Moats pulled the door open and gazed into the van. He gaged at what he saw and stood to the side and vomited a little bit.

"This shit is out of control," Moats stated, bent over spewing.

Moats spit and cleared his throat as Simmons stepped closer.

"You alright?"

"I`m good. I aint seen this much blood since Fallujah…shit."

Simmons looked inside. Jolene and Archie were on top of one another covered in blood. Archie`s body was missing its hands, with the jugular cut jagged. His face was slashed with tiny cuts all over, and his right eye was outside the socket. He was beyond recognition. Jolene was folded up on top of Archie with a large surgical scalpel plunged precisely into the center of her heart. Her eyes were wide open.

"This brutal shit is unnecessary," Simmons muttered sadly.

Moats swung the door open wider as Simmons looked closer.

"My God…what are we in partner?"

Simmons slammed the van door shut and the two detectives walked a few feet away. Simmons placed a call on his radio for back-up and the coroner. Moats sat on the steps of the funeral home and put his head in his hands. Simmons finished his call and looked toward the street in front of the funeral parlor. A navy-blue Buick with two white men rolled through slowly and peered at the two detectives.

"Moats," Simmons bellowed loudly as he pulled his gun.

Moats sprung from the stairs startled and glanced at Simmons who was focused on the Buick. Moats pulled his gun quickly and aimed at the Buick.

"POLICE!" Moats shouted at the car.

The two men in the car looked at the detectives and drove away quickly as Moats darted toward the intersection pointing his gun. The car picked up speed and peeled away down the street and made a quick left. Moats trotted back to the front of the building.

"What the fuck was that?" Simmons boasted.

"Government fucking tags H, what the hell is going on…shit man!" Moats swore.

• • •

"We definitely can't go back to the station…we don't know who's in on this situation along with Gaines."

"We are out here on our own gentlemen. If your captain is a part of the group, they have inside information on everything up to this point…the bodies in my district, yours and everywhere are probably tied to this group, hell…my superiors might be in on it too… if all our facts line up… We need to break this situation open… The way to do that is to go directly to 4090 Delaware…see for ourselves what's down there…find out what's going on, and who is really behind this crazy shit."

Detective Johns looked at Simmons, Moats and the two detectives he had with him. They stood in front of the diner near Broad and Wharton streets talking, sharing information and formulating a plan.

"Maybe we should just grab Detective Gaines and smack the shit outta 'her for info," Moats suggested.

"If this is what our witnesses say it is…she aint going without a fight. I've known her for over ten years. Worked cases with her, and now it's come to this."

"This group is all powerful…who knows how far up the chain this crap goes. If we are gonna do it…we go dark… all in."

"We've come too far to turn back now…our lives are on the line."

"H…what about pimp boys' Demetrius' family?"

"We owe him a favor, but, it's going to have to wait. He did murder a woman, at least one for sure that we know of…aside from that, if we're about to go to war, we need to get heavier iron…protect us first."

"I'll go by the 1st district and load up a few things. We can meet back here tonight to finalize everything," Johns instructed.

"Eight o'clock sharp…no radio contact until then," Simmons advised.

• • •

As the strange murders accumulated throughout the city of Philadelphia, the evening news broadcasts all around Philadelphia were transmitting stories about the dozens of missing women and young black men as, individual disappearance cases with no connection to one another. In the manner of the bodies turning up mutilated, a broadcast station alleged that the city had a 'serial slasher' who revered dismembering people. One radio station reported the story as a 'Crazy cult,' kidnapping group, going about recruiting individuals for their satanic mission of killing underprivileged people and the homeless. The murder of Sherry Campbell, found dead in a hotel freezer was still unsolved, and it was attributed to the serial slasher, who had found a young vulnerable woman to prey on. At the Henry funeral parlor on 54th street, the crime was termed a robbery gone bad. The brutality in Franklin square of a rich white woman, was a headline on the front of the daily newspapers. A part time 'Handy man' for the Hoffman's was charged and accused of slaughtering Gretchen Hoffman. Her still missing husband, Erwin J. Hoffman, was considered an accomplice and a put on the FBI's most wanted list of fugitives.

The entire city was put on guard. Every suburb, every hood, and in every part of Philadelphia, everyone was on a frightened readiness of high alert. Communities of people were boiling over with suspicion, watching and waiting vigilantly, arming themselves to protect, while waiting to see what was approaching next.

...

IN MOUNT AIRY

    Albert Boykins, from Boykins funeral services in mount airy was driving along north Broad street with his son Albert junior. They`d rented a mid-sized U-Haul truck. The sun was just about to break the sky and they had cleaned out the remaining bodies that Albert senior had worked on for organ harvesting. He`d gotten word from the other surgeons who went to the emergency meeting at 4090 Delaware. Only, Albert chose not to attend. Instead, he starting cleaning his funeral home and closed down his business. Albert senior and his son drove into north Philly looking for vacant lots with overgrown grass and shrubs. Albert senior pulled the truck up to a corner near Erie avenue and Pike streets. He shut the truck engine off and turned the headlights off. He and his son Albert junior put on black gloves and pulled their hoodies over their heads. They exited the truck looking around and no one was moving. They opened the rear of the truck and pulled a large grey storage container out. The container was wrapped heavily in plastic wrap. They lugged the container quickly into the brush and sat it down. The container hit the ground with a weighty clunk. The two men walked quickly back to the truck and locked the back door and drove away leaving the container behind in the brush barely visible from the street…

    Albert junior was behind the wheel as the two men sped through south Philly across Wharton street. Albert senior looked at his watch and up at the sky.

    "It's getting light outside…21st and Wharton, it's an empty lot there."

Albert junior pressed the gas. Several minutes later they arrived at 21st and Wharton and parked the truck. They looked down Wharton and a woman was walking toward the corner. They waited for the woman to walk past and they put their gloves on again and exited the truck. They opened the back door and dragged out their last of three containers and muscled it into the overgrown brush in a lot. Albert junior accidently tore a hole in the plastic wrap they had heavily covered the blue container with. Albert junior quickly pulled up brush and weeds from around the container and tossed it on top trying to cover the tear.

    "Let's go son. There`s no time for that."

The two men hustled back to the van and shut the doors. They jumped in and drove away quickly down 21st street.

    "Pop…you think Demetrius gonna snitch, and give us up?"

    "I really don't know son…he`s a drug dealer who is capable of anything…we are leaving town though, until we find out which way the wind is going to blow…and there is no us if it comes down to it… It's all on me son, I'll take the fall."

In Springfield Township on Walnut Lane

Braheem pulled his car to the shoulder of the road on Walnut lane after having just made a right turn off Ogden avenue. He questioned himself asking if he turned too fast as he lowered his car radio. The flashing police headlights behind him caught him by surprise. Braheem quickly reached into his glove box and pulled the car registration out and sat it on the dash in front of his steering wheel. He cracked the driver's side window and put his hands on the steering wheel and watched the troopers approaching on both sides of his car through the rear-view mirror. He looked around for eye witnesses and no one was there. His car was stalled near a tree lined area next to a dense wooded area. The two troopers approached his car, one on either side. Braheem turned to his left as the officer approached the window.

"What's up…where you headed?"

"I'm going to work…I work at the Springfield mall."

"You know why we pulled you over?"

"I got a broken tail light, I'm getting some red tape to put on it tonight…I need to inform you that I have a firearm on me, and I'm licensed to carry."

"Let me see you driver's license, registration, and gun permit…put your car in park."

Braheem passed the driver side trooper his registration through the crack in his window.

"Is my light the reason you stopped me? I'm getting it fixed, just going to work at -"

"Nobody owes you an explanation," the trooper interrupted with tone.

The trooper at the right side of the car unholstered his gun. Braheem stopped talking and kept his composure.

"What's your name boy, and where is the identification I asked for?"

"It's in my wallet…in my back pocket, I'm going to reach for it now," responded Braheem annoyed."

Braheem reached forward and turned his cell phone camera on and started recording.

"What you do that for…I asked you for your identification," the trooper shouted.

Braheem slid forward in his seat and moved his hand slowly toward his back pocket. He took his wallet out with his right hand and dropped it accidently between his knees. His handgun was on his hip and visible when he leaned forward to pick up his wallet. He reached to pick it up and the trooper to his right fired two shots through the closed passenger side window, hitting Braheem in his shoulder and chest. Braheem slid down in his seat with his wallet in his hand and cringed in agony. The passenger side trooper broke out the window, reached inside and unlocked the door. He grabbed the holstered hand gun off Braheem's hip. Braheem struggled for air as he looked at the trooper who shot him. Braheem grabbed the troopers wrist with what little strength he had left and the trooper shoved his hand away. The trooper took Braheem's wallet and pushed it back into his hip pocket. Braheem took his final breaths scowling at the smiling trooper. The trooper placed Braheem's gun in his right hand and closed his fist. The trooper took the cellphone, stopped the recording and deleted it. He threw the cell phone into the brush and the two troopers walked slowly back to their car and called in the shooting.

"Shots fired, shots fired…officer needs assistance, black male shot…"

They placed road flares behind the car and turned on their hazard flashers as they waited for patrols and an ambulance to arrive. Five minutes later a sergeant arrived on the scene and asked the troopers what happened.

"We pulled the guy over, and he reached for and pulled out his gun."

The ambulance EMT's pronounced Braheem deceased at the scene and loaded his body into the ambulance.

• • •

At the Donut shop, Broad street and Olney Avenue

The SEPTA station was busy with bus travelers and pedestrians exiting the subway undergrounds heading toward buses waiting at the terminal. Transportation police were strolling about the bus stop where the 26-bus picked up riders headed north into Germantown. Gypsy taxi drivers strolled about whispering, "Hack man," under their breath to women with children, and the elderly. Several hustlers did hand to hand weed sales transactions right under the noses of the transit police. Rodney was inside the donut shop arguing with the store attendant about his order not being fresh. The attendant threatened to call the police because Rodney was becoming belligerent, shouting at the cashiers and potential customers.

"This food stale as shit!" "I want my money back!"

Rodney threw his bag of food at a cashier hitting her in the face. The cashier ran around the counter and rushed at Rodney who shoved her to the floor. The young woman jumped up and kicked at Rodney and threw a couple punches that didn't land. A co-worker in the donut shop jumped the counter and punched Rodney in the back of his head. Rodney spun around quickly and started throwing dagger like punches at the co-worker. The two men went blow for blow, fists landing, chest, in chin, at jaw, and eyes. The manager of the donut shop jumped in and broke the two young men apart just as the police rushed in. The officers grabbed Rodney and slammed him to the floor.

"What the fuck y'all only grabbing me for!" Rodney shouted. "They swung on me first!"

"That's what you get pussy!" shouted the girl cashier.

The male cashier was clearing his mouth of blood with napkins as the officers asked what happened while trying to handcuff Rodney who was struggling to turn himself face up on the floor.

"Stop resisting," Shouted the officer as he put his knee in Rodney's back.

The other officer put his hands at the back of Rodney's head and pressed down, putting his full weight on Rodney's face.

"I can't breathe," Rodney uttered struggling to get air.

The officers cuffed him and rolled him over on his back.

"This asshole came in here and threw his food in the face of my employee."

"Fuck y'all!" shouted Rodney. "Y'all always serving old stale shit."

"Officers…he come in here every day, complaining about the same thing, dickhead."

The officers looked at the girl cashier and hustled Rodney outside toward the patrol car. A crowd of onlookers watched as Rodney struggled in his cuffs as the officers pushed him into the backseat of their car faced down. They slammed the car door and returned to the store and wrote an incident report. They returned to the car outside and Rodney was screaming obscenities and kicking the inside of the rear right window with both feet.

"Kick that window one more time and I'm putting you in leg chains."

Rodney kicked the window with both feet again and the window shattered, splintering the glass as it remained in the frame of the door.

"Fuck you man…why you aint locking them up?" Rodney shouted.

The officer reached into the back seat and dragged Rodney out to the ground. The crowd of onlookers pulled out their cell phones, started to record and let out a gasp of 'oohs' and 'aahs.' The officer pulled a set of leg shackles out of the trunk and clamped them on Rodney's legs. He and the other officer lifted the cussing, spitting, and screaming Rodney from the ground and shoved him into the rear of the police car again. They slammed the door and drove away…

The officers drove Rodney to the parking lot driveway at Central high school two blocks down Olney avenue. They parked at the rear out of sight behind the building and started beating

Rodney in his chest and neck with their batons. Rodney screamed out for help and one of the officers punched him in his jaw. Rodney passed out from the hard blow. The other officers reached over and choked Rodney at this throat, pressing down for nearly three minutes. Rodney's body convulsed from lack of air and went limp shortly after. The officer pinched Rodney's nose and held it closed for another two minutes as his partner covered his mouth. They held Rodney in that position for another three minutes. Rodney's body was limp and lifeless. The officers let go of his face and Rodney was motionless and his body slumped over in the back seat. The driver side officer opened the car door and took the leg restraints off Rodney and sat him upright again and opened his eyes. He slapped Rodney a couple times on his face in a weak attempt to revive him. Rodney wasn't breathing. The officer climbed back into the front seat and the two officers drove slowly to the 35th district police station. They pulled Rodney out of the car and laid him on his back and started doing chest compressions. The other officer called for an ambulance and a heart defibrillator from inside the police station and walked back to Rodney's body.

"Did you hear about Moats…and Simmons," asked the officer doing chest compressions.

"I heard…they deserve whatever they get. Race trader Simmons and especially that nigger Moats," stated the other officer.

"Fuck'um both."

A couple officers came out of the building carrying the heart defibrillator to assist and asked what happened.

"We arrested this guy for assault in a fight up at Broad and Olney…looks like he panicked and went into cardiac arrest or something… ambulance is in route."

• • •

GERMANTOWN

Word spread rapidly that the mayor, the assistant district attorney and the police commissioner would be in attendance answering questions about the increased rash of missing persons, the mysterious deaths of Sherry Elise Campbell, and Sabrina 'Shine' Minshew, the mutilated body found in the basement on Porter street.

All the major news outlets and radio stations were set up there on the lawn area beneath the tennis courts at Ardleigh and Haines street. The lawn area was crowded with nearly a thousand people from surrounding neighborhoods and other areas in the city. People wanted answers from the authorities about what was going on, and who they could hold responsible for the horrific crimes happening. Parts of the crowd were community activists, holding skyward, homemade signs for 'Justice.' Others were chanting the names of missing loved ones and the names Sherry Campbell, and Sabrina Minshew rang out in the crowd.

Melody and Noah were standing next to Tyriq, mixed in with the crowd of people. Fiona's parents, Yousef and Carolyn Middleton were guest speakers, as well as a few other parents with missing children and family members.

"I assure you all that we are using all of our resources to catch those responsible for the crimes in our communities…we are in the process of establishing a new task force to investigate the mysterious murders," explained the mayor. "At this time I'd like to turn the platform over to the commissioner to answer your specific questions concerning the missing persons."

The mayor stepped away from the microphone and the commissioner stepped in front.

"Thank you Mr. mayor…I'm going to make a few statements and then take questions…first, we are still gathering investigative clues on all of our open cases concerning missing persons, and the murder of miss Fiona Middleton and miss Sabrina Minshew…just to name a few."

"Tell us who kidnapping our peoples," a man shouted from the crowd angrily.

The angry man received a few "That's rights, and Hell yea!" cosigns from others in the crowd.

"Sir…we are investigating a few organizations,' but we won't be divulging specific names of groups in question, or under investigation," countered the commissioner.

"Why`you here then!" a different man shouted. "Is a serial slasher out here, yes or no!"

"We are looking into the strange events of missing organs in the for mentioned cases…that's all I can say about that," responded the commissioner.

"As the mayor stated, we are developing a task force of our best investigating officers to handle the matters at hand. When we get more information we will inform the families, and the communities about the facts, until then, everyone should remain calm and let us do our jobs."

The commissioner stepped away from the microphone visibly frustrated and trying hard to maintain composure. The assistant district attorney stepped to the front amid boos from sections in the crowd.

"Friends, Brothers and Sisters…I feel, we`eee should hear, from our families in need of support at this moment, please, please… a moment of respect, please… First let me introduce you to the head instructor of the special investigative task force the commissioner just mentioned, detective Nelly Gaines from the 35th district police station. She has over a decade of experience in these types of crimes and will be a supreme leader…I assure you."

The assistant district attorney pointed at detective Nelly Gaines and she waived her hand to the crowd.

Alright, now let us welcome, Mr. Middleton and his lovely wife. They are the`ee parents of Fiona Middleton."

The assistant district attorney stepped aside and welcomed the Middleton`s. The crowd of onlookers applauded.

"My daughter was a kind, and loving young woman…she loved everyone…she worked hard in school…she is my only child…I miss her soooo much," Carolyn Middletown," divulged emotionally. Yousef Middleton comforted his wife as she broke emotionally.

"If anyone has information about my daughter, please speak with the police," mumbled Yousef.

The Middletown's stepped away and the assistant district attorney stepped back in front.

"Brothers and Sisters…it is our responsibility to do our best, to hold one another up in time of need…we`ee thank the Middleton family for their courage to speak out about their lovely child Fiona…and we`ee support them whole heartedly…rest assured that the office of the district attorney will support and convict all those involved in any matter concerning the murder, or disappearance of our fine citizens…we`ee thank you for coming out today, and remember…we`ee are more diligent if working together."

The assistant district attorney whispered in the ear of the mayor and walked away with two suit dressed security guards and detective Gaines walking with him to his car. The mayor returned to the microphone and took more questions from the agitated crowd.

•••

2500 west Norris Street. Johnson Homes

The sun was going down and it was business as usually at the weed spot in building 2514. Customers streamed in and out of the house purchasing their favorite strands of marijuana. Dip sat at a small kitchen table putting quarter ounces of weed in containers. Standing near the front door of the small house was a young thug with a pistol in his hand letting customers in and out of the door. Dip had a shotgun leaning on the table and a large duffle bag seated on the floor filled with pounds of weed. The house was empty inside except for the table, two chairs and the two men inside. Dip stopped and counted money from his last ten transactions and put a rubber band around it. He stuffed the money in a black backpack hanging on the back of one of the chairs.

"This shit is movin' like it's free…we gone' be done by midnight," Dip confirmed.

"Good tree always sell itself," responded the doorway guarding thug.

"Check the youngins outside."

The thug moved toward the front window of the house and peered out a tattered curtain shade.

"They on post."

"Ai'ight…gotta piss, don't let nobody in till I come back down."

Dip stood up and walked up stairs to the bathroom and the thug cracked the front door and stuck his head out.

"Y'all straight out here?"

"On chill," one of the young lookouts responded.

"Ai'ight…we gone' order pizzas in a few."

The thug shut the front door and locked it as the lookouts nodded in agreement. The thug walked through the house and looked out the rear window. Nothing was moving. He checked the locks on the back door securing them. As he strolled back to the front Dip walked down the front stairs.

"We good?"

"Solid as a rock Dip."

"Roll one up niggah," Dip instructed as he sat back at the table.

The thug stepped away from the door and sat his pistol on the table. He reached inside the backpack and pulled out blunt wraps and started crushing weed and rolling blunts…

Outside the house the two lookouts continued watching for suspicious and unfamiliar customers. A few yards away near the corner of the projects, seated on a fire hydrant was another lookout watching approaching, and passing cars. The lookout saw a black van pull up to the corner of Norris and two black men exit wearing water department uniforms and work boots. They strolled past the corner lookout who lowered his head and played around on his cell phone as the two men headed toward 2514 with their hands inside their jumpsuits. The lookout glanced up at the two men looking them up and down.

"Where is unit 2518, Debra Melton's, you know her, where she lives," asked one of the men.

"Umm…she stay in 2518 I think…walk to da'other side a'dem cribs straight back," responded the young corner lookout.

"Thanks."

The two men walked up the pathway toward 2514. As they continued past the corner hustler, he shoved his phone in his blue jeans, and raised both arms in the air like an air traffic controller on a navy ship signaling to a jet pilot. He got the attention of the two young hustlers sitting in front of 2514 who watched the two men walking toward them from afar. The corner lookout raised five fingers on his right hand, and closed his left fist in a circle. He made the motion twice and ran down Norris street quickly. The two hustlers in front of 2514 stood up and calmly banged on the front window of the house three times. The shade of the house lifted in the corner and one of the lookouts mimicked the same gesture as the corner lookout. Five fingers and a fist. The two lookouts dispersed quickly. One of them walked left rapidly down the pathway and the other one went right and disappeared behind the building. The moved in unison and were both dressed in white t-shirts and blue jeans. The two men in water department uniforms walked up to 2514 and stopped watching the two lookouts as they dispersed around the sides of the buildings. The two men looked left, then right, searching for 2518. The front door of 2514 swung open and Dip stepped out holding a 20-gauge shotgun. He chambered a round and shouted at the two men.

"Y'all picked the wrong spot…you think it's sweet!" Dip cautioned pointing the shotgun at the two men.

The two men froze and took a step rearward into a defensive position.

"Wait!" shouted one of the men. "We're looking for 2518!"

They looked left, then right and saw three other young hustlers all dressed in white t-shirts and jeans along with the two lookouts with hand guns coming toward them from the right side from behind building 2514. The group of hustlers started shooting in the direction of the two men. Dip pulled the trigger on the shotgun. It left off a blast that echoed off the walls of the homes rattling windows. The two men rolled to the ground and pulled out hands guns of their own and started to return gunfire at Dip in the doorway, and the flanking hustlers who started ducking beside buildings and dumpsters as they left off round after round in the direction of the two men with their handguns. Dip ducked back inside the framing of the doorway. After firing ten to fifteen rounds the group of hustlers ran toward the space between 2516 and disappeared into the dark alleyway between the houses. Dip fired two more blasts from the doorway with the shotgun. He emptied the shotgun and the two men climbed to their feet and retreated down the path the same way they'd entered as Dip started a reload. As they reached the end of the path, the corner lookout popped out from behind a parked car with two others young thugs. They opened fire on the two men from the left side. The two men returned fire as they ran in the opposite direction to the right toward their van. The two men gun shots bounced of cars and windshields missing their marks. Shots sounds reverberated into the open sky. Screams could be heard from surrounding buildings as the shots echoed in the atmosphere like fireworks on the fourth of July. The corner lookout and his group ran along the parked cars, ducking behind each one as they passed, firing round after round, flanking the two men running toward their van. One of the two men took a round to the back and collapsed to the ground. The other man looked back, fired two more rounds over his shoulder and continued running as fast as he could zig zagging up the sidewalk. The corner lookout and his crew stopped firing and sprinted into the opposite direction alongside the parked cars and down 25th street and into darkness. The remaining man made it to the black van and jumped inside. He started the van and rolled the window down looking around frantically. He slid down in his seat and anxiously changed the clip in his gun, put the van in drive and sped down the street along the parked cars with his gun pointed out the window looking for the thugs who opened fire on him. Nothing or no one was moving. He sped away down 25th street leaving his comrade on the side walk.

A full two minutes passed and the front door of 2514 opened. Dip ran down the pathway with the black backpack on and a Glock in his hand. The two front door lookouts, and the corner hydrant lookout ran up from different directions.

"Nobody got hit right?"

"Naw, err'body good Dip," one of the young lookouts said breathing rapidly.

"I popped one of um…he laid out," the corner hydrant lookout assured.

The group trotted toward the man lying on the ground halfway up 25th street. They stood over him assuring he was dead.

"Told you Dip," the corner lookout affirmed.

"He definitely gone," responded Dip. "Get rid of them hammers…go meet P at the other trap spot…he got the duffle with the work in it."

Dip bent over the body and pushed the man over and removed the man's baseball hat. He looked closely at the man's eyes that were still open. Dip went through the dead man's overall pockets quickly. He pulled out the man's wallet, opened it quickly, looked at his identification, and threw it on the ground next to the body.

"Yo…he five O."

He gazed at the man's face and neck and pulled a full mask off the man's face. The dead man was white and wearing a brown lifelike facemask making him appear to be African American.

"What the fuck is this bullshit," Dip questioned uncertainly.

"That's some crazy shit," added the corner lookout as police sirens echoed from a few blocks away.

"Bounce…get rid of those hammers…go get P, I`ll hit y`all in a week," Dip instructed.

Dip sprinted down 25th street and the hustlers bolted into the building area and disappeared behind 2516 into the darkness of the alleyways…

Detective Harrison drove the black van through the back streets of North Philly speeding toward the 35th district. He threw his Glock pistol out the window, drove a few more feet and threw his hat out into the street. He peeled off his facemask and his gloves. He threw them into the street. He got far enough away from the scene and stopped at a red light near Wyoming and pulled out his cell phone.

"The shit went bad…real fast…we never got to Debra Melton…Rucker is down at the scene…some fucking… kid criminals' with guns opened up on us…a Fucking ambush!"

• • •

Simmons, Moats, Johns and two other detectives stood at the trunk of detective Johns squad car. The detectives finalized their plan on how they were going to approach 4090 Delaware avenue. All the detectives added bullet proof vests, extra gun clips and long guns to their arsenal of gear. Simmons shouldered a 20-gauge shotgun, and an extra Glock along with his revolver. Moats strapped an extra pistol to his ankle holster and loaded five extra AR-15 magazine clips to his belt harness. The men loaded into three cars and started toward 4090. As they started away, the call about 2500 Norris street came across the police dispatch radio.

"That's where pimp boys' momma lives…Johnson homes."

"Right…change of plans," Simmons responded.

"An officer is down?" vacillated Moats listening closely to the call.

"Our day can`t possibly get any stranger than it has been."

Moats called Johns on his walkie and let them know they were headed to the Johnson homes address before they convened on 4090 Delaware avenue.

• • •

The cars with Moats and Simmons, and Johns and his detective squad pulled up to the Johnsons homes housing projects. As they parked sporadically and exited they saw Detective Gaines speeding away from the scene in a car with Detective Harrison riding in the passenger seat. They gazed at the car making eye contact with Gaines who sped away. The scene was covered with duty police, detectives from the district and neighbors watching to see what was going on. An ambulance was on scene waiting for the detectives to finish documenting the scene. Moats, Simmons and Johns walked over.

"What happened here?" Simmons questioned addressing the crowd of onlookers.

Moats immediately started up the path after scoping the building numbers that started with 2010. Debra Melton's 2018 was in his mind.

"Muh'fucker got lit up, comin'round wearing a black man face…robbin'da wrong muh'fucker."

Simmons looked at the man and made his way toward the body. On the ground was detective Rucker with a full faced mask of a black man lying next to him on the ground near his wallet. Detectives were examining his body and marking off gun shell casing rounds in the area. Moats continued walking through the projects and scattered onlookers.

"Anybody seen Mrs. Melton from 2018. She aint out here is she?"

None of the onlookers responded to Moats. Moats continued past, walking up and by 2016 and walked to the rear of the buildings until he reached 2018. As he approached the door he heard a dog barking viciously from inside. He knocked on the door of 2018 and a female voice echoed through over the barking.

"Who is it?"

"It's the police…open up please."

"Who?"

"Police…detective Moats."

The door cracked open and a teenaged girl was inside peeping out. The girl opened the door with her right hand behind her back. She swung the door all the way and Moats looked past the teenaged girl and a woman was seated in a chair in the living room area. A large pit-bull growled at Moats continuously. The teenaged girl grabbed the dog in the collar.

"Mrs. Melton?"

"What you want officer…I'ont know nothing about my son and his crazy business."

Moats stepped completely inside the house and shut the door behind him and locked it. The dog growled louder as Moats stepped in and lifted his hands so the dog could see them. The teenage girl let go of the dog and the growling animal took to steps toward Moats ready to attack. The girl gave a command.

"Go sit with momma," the teenage girl uttered.

The dog stopped growling and walked slowly toward Mrs. Melton and sat next to her chair and stared at Moats. The teenaged girl put her hands on her hips and looked at Moats waiting.

"I'm detective Moats…you, and your daughter are in serious danger."

Mrs. Melton stood up from her chair. The dog stood up next to her.

"How are we in danger?" asked Mrs. Melton concerned.

She moved toward Moats and the dog followed.

"Has anyone been here looking for you?"

"You answer my question, with a question…Nobody been here…who looking for me?"

"We have strong reason to believe some dangerous people who want to hurt your son Demetrius, will come looking for you as well…I think you and your family should leave."

"I aint going nowhere Mr. my family been here thirty years…we aint leaving."

"Who are these people you talking about," asked the teenaged girl concerned.

"A white supremacist group…we suspect."

"So y'all don't even really know who it is?"

"We are still putting information together, but these people are deadly serious…we think they were coming tonight. Did you hear the shooting tonight?"

Mrs. Melton looked at Moats with a blank stare. Moats saw that same gaze on Demetrius before.

"We heard the shooting, and, we shoot back around here," the teenaged girl verified.

"We can't force you to leave, but your son asked us to come make sure you were okay…he was the one actually concerned."

"So what's gonna happen to my brother…is he gonna be safe…in jail?"

Moats hesitated.

"I can't really say yes…he is facing serious murder charges though."

"We aint leaving officer… aint nowhere to go…this is home." Mrs. Melton said assuredly as she took her seat again.

The teenaged girl started toward the front door. As she moved Moats nodded to Mrs. Melton. He turned and followed. The teenaged girl had a Glock shoved into her waistband near her spine.

"When I see your son, I'll tell him you both are okay."

"Thanks for telling us," the teenaged girl said as she unlocked the front door.

Moats exited the house and heard the door lock behind him. He walked back down the path heading toward the crime scene.

...

Simmons stood with detective Johns waiting, as Moats walked down the path. The EMT's were putting detective Rucker's covered body in the back of the ambulance. Moats looked around at the dozens of yellow markers covering shell casings scattered everywhere.

"Was she there, and alive?"

"She was there H…with her daughter, a Taurus pistol and a vicious pit-bull…all in one piece, saying they aint going nowhere."

"I guess that's that…we get word to Demetrius about his mother. We kept our obligation."

"Not sure if they understood clearly who these people are…hell, I don't even really know, but, a dog and a gun might not get the job done."

"What's the move gents…they gotta know we're coming by now," detective Johns questioned.

"Let's get to the bottom of it then," Simmons replied.

The detectives started toward their cars.

"Who was it on the ground H?"

"Our former colleague, detective Rucker, dressed as a DPW guy…with a covering mask making him look…black."

Moats looked at Simmons with a repulsed stare as the two men climbed into the car.

"Now these bastards in black face masks, so my people can get the blame?" "Is Gaines, Harrison…and dead Rucker, possibly behind most of this shit?"

Moats continued his gaze of disgust at Simmons who remained quiet while shaking his head confused.

"Nothing to say huh H?" Moats stated annoyed.

"Speechless partner."

Simmons sat quietly staring at the road as they drove toward the expressway.

...

Simmons parked the car at the edge of the roadway a few yards from the front entrance of 4090 Delaware. Detective Johns drove to the opposite end of the roadway, made a U-turn and parked in the middle of the two-way street near the curb. Moats exited the car before the group could execute their plan.

"Moats…what are you doing, stick to the plan!" Simmons shouted from the car window.

"Fuck this, it's time to hunt…I'm tired of these muther'fuckers!"

Moats walked aggressively toward the front gates of the warehouse at 4090. He had pistol in his hand with his assault rifle strapped to his back in a shoulder harness. Simmons exited the car as quickly as he could heading to back up his partner. Simmons waved toward detective Johns and he exited his car followed by detectives Barnes and McMillian. Moats strolled directly up to the front gate and peered through the green fencing. He couldn't see inside clearly. The sky above the plant was clouded with a mist of light ash that was drifting toward the river. Moats stepped reward and looked up at a security camera that was bolted to the wall. The camera was pointed toward the parking area facing away from the fence. As Moats stepped rearward, the camera turned slowly toward him.

"What the hell happened to waiting for the gate to open," Johns asked rushing up.

"I say we climb the gate and introduce ourselves," proposed Moats angrily.

The group of men questioned Moats tactics visually and quickly realized that they were already in deep water. Johns, Simmons and detectives McMillian and Barnes took defensive positions guarding the two-way street looking left then right. Simmons motioned for the attention of Moats who was just about to start climbing the fence.

"Headlights coming," Simmons cautioned grabbing Moats by the arm.

Moats took his foot out of the fencing and stepped backward away from the front gate. Simmons moved to the side and raised his shotgun pointing at the front facing fencing. The front gate crashed open violently toward the curb and restricted the view of Simmons. Simmons was struck by the crashing fence and knocked rearward to the ground. He was now behind the open gate bleeding from his forehead. A large tarp covered dump truck pulled out from inside. Moats retreated backward and was standing near the curb pointing his gun at the two men inside. He glanced quickly at Simmons who was struggling to get back on his feet. The driver of the truck saw Moats standing in the roadway and pressed the gas pedal on the truck. The truck barreled toward Moats picking up speed. Moats started firing his pistol at the driver's side of the truck as he stepped double time in reverse out of the path of the moving truck. Simmons climbed to one knee, and from behind the gate, he fired two shotgun blasts at the passenger side door. Moats rolled to his left side on the ground and retreated out of the way of the truck. Johns, Barnes and McMillian volleyed shots at the engine block and tires from across the roadway. Two ar-15 carrying security guards rushed from inside the gated area and fired upon the detectives from the edges of the fencing. Moats climbed to his feet and sprinted toward their parked car. He knelt behind the front tire and raised his ar-15 and left off a barrage of covering fire rounds as Simmons stood up and back peddled his way slowly away from the fence he was behind. The two security guards fired in the direction of Johns, Barnes and McMillian who were exposed. They never saw Simmons directly to their right behind the fence. Johns dropped to the ground, straddled himself to the asphalt and fired rounds as rapidly as he could. Return fire bounced all around him kicking up chunks of asphalt by his head and face. Barnes and McMillian, the two detectives flanking his right were caught in a hail of fire from the remaining security guard as well as the driver of the truck who started firing a pistol from the driver's side window of the truck directly at Barnes and McMillian. The driver fired his semi-automatic, with his foot still on the trucks gas pedal, letting rounds go until the cylinder stopped and his clip was empty. The driver of the truck took a shot to the shoulder from the Barnes but never took his foot off the gas pedal. The truck rolled directly toward Johns who was straddling the ground. The truck rolled directly over top of John's who laid as flat as he could as the truck slammed against two concrete pillars directly opposite the front entrance of 4090. The force of the truck vibrated the ground and slightly lifted the rear of the truck while trapping Johns underneath. The two armed security guards walked forward into the street firing shots. One walked toward Moats, and the other reloaded his ar-15 and rushed toward Barnes and McMillian. One guard dropped to one knee in the roadway and fired several rounds hitting detective Barnes in his chest protector, neck and right shoulder. Barnes crumbled to the street and wriggled his way toward the side area of the truck beneath the driver's side door screaming.

"I'm hit…I'm hit!"

Moats was returning fire. His shots landed true, striking the advancing guard in his ribs. The guard fell to the ground. Simmons rushed from behind the fencing area flanking the remaining guard. Simmons blasted the guard in his back with a shotgun round. The guard fell forward to the asphalt. The medley of shots stopped and McMillian rushed over to the truck and helped the wounded detective Barnes who was bleeding profusely. He glanced under the truck momentarily and Johns rolled from underneath covered in black grime and fluid leaking from the truck. Moats rushed up to the passenger side and yanked open truck door pointing his pistol inside. The truck passenger was dressed in black coveralls. He rolled from the passenger side with a large section of his arm and ribs gushing blood. He hit the ground with a heavy thud. Moats climbed through the cab area and pointed his pistol in the face of the driver who was still conscious and leaning forward on the steering wheel with his spent pistol in his hand, bleeding from his face and neck. Moats punched the driver with his pistol and shouted.

"Get the fuck out!"

"Help," the driver mumbled.

Moats pushed the driver out of the seat. The driver tumbled out of the seat and hit the ground face first nearly landing on Barnes and McMillian. Moats climbed through the truck cab to the other side and jumped out. Simmons trotted toward the wounded detective holding his face and calling for help on the walkie talkie. Detective Johns helped McMillian by putting pressure on Barnes` chest wound as McMillian performed CPR chest compressions. Moats looked on and started kicking the driver of the truck in his torso as the driver begged for help. Simmons reached the other side of the truck and grabbed Moats wrapping his arms around him.

"It`s over got dammit!" Simmons shouted at Moats in a chastising tone.

"It aint over! fuck that," Moats countered kicking at the bleeding driver.

Simmons shoved Moats in mid-kick and Moats lost his balance and fell to the ground.

"ITS FUCKING OVER!" Simmons shouted. "This shit happens when you get reckless…we had a got damned plan!"

Moats watched quietly as Johns stopped the chest compressions and McMillian discontinued CPR. Simmons walked over to the driver of the truck, yanked his arm and handcuffed him to the front bumper of the truck as the driver pleaded for help while writhing in pain. Moats stood to his feet as a fleet of unmarked police cars, police vans and ambulances' sped down the roadway toward 4090 with their lights flashing. The above area lit up from the sky as two helicopters appeared overhead shining bright beams of light as they circled the plant. The unmarked cars screeched to a stop and federal agents jumped from the cars shouting instructions at the detectives.

"DROP YOUR WEAPONS!"

The detectives laid their guns on the ground and raised their hands skyward…

…

"So who`s idea was it to go Rambo on this warehouse?" asked the FBI director seething.

Johns, Moats, Simmons and McMillian didn't say a word.

"You assholes screwed up a four-year investigation. We`ve been gathering intel on this nationwide group, who has been terrorizing communities of color, hell bent on exterminating minorities…this shit is so immense and you have no idea, the level of people and departments and places the FBI and CIA have been trying to string all the bullshit…including your Captain Gaines…hundreds, maybe thousands of others involved in the group…And now, thanks to you trigger happy jackasses…everybody in the Philadelphia chapter is in the wind…and all we have is this fiasco, four dead bad guys, a dead detective and a bunch or corpses…all on your watch…fuck-ups."

The FBI director started away from the entryway of the plant and strolled inside the warehouse.

"Fuck you!" shouted Moats. "If y'all had it figured out…what took you so long to make a move?"

The FBI director stopped in the doorway of the plant and turned around. He gazed at Moats and the rest of the detectives. He motioned toward one of his agents and whispered instruction. The agent motioned to several other agents nearby and they approached Moats, Simmons, Johns and McMillian and arrested them. The group of detectives were zip tied and led away outside the plant toward unmarked FBI vehicle's…

The FBI director strolled through 4090 giving directions to his remaining agents on scene as they surveyed the area for evidence. Every trace of the KOTGC was gone except for a few pamphlets, armbands and the dead bodies they left behind. He walked toward the area where the large generators were and saw close to ten bodies piled in front of Furness three. The bodies were mutilated, some missing skin and exposing decaying flesh, others stapled shut on their torso areas, heads shaved clean of hair, and separated limbs rotting. Amongst the pile of corpses was doctor Erwin J Hoffman's remains with his hands missing. His torso was a strange color of purple with bruising in the rib areas. Several of the bodies had gapping mouths, as if they were trying to shout out for help that never arrived and their mouths froze from anguish. Others had bulging eyes glossy, staring…focused on nothing.

The entire scene was a desecration of humanity. The bodies were well past dead, yet, the sounds of pain, weariness and struggle echoed from their devastated bodies. The Furness was still burning and small plumes of ash was drifting out through the chimney gently sprinkling itself in the river. The FBI director covered his face with a handkerchief trying to combat the odor of death. He looked around at the chaos of remains, and the trash in the warehouse…he walked toward a different section of the plant with a tear welling up in his eye.

...

FOUR MONTHS LATER

The thin man sat at his desk in his large chair talking on the telephone.

"The`ee next wave of extermination is already underway…the biological weapon has been deployed in a wet market in China…it`s perfect because this type of thing has happened there in China previously…they`ll never get it under control in time…we will certainly lose some, but make certain, our true brothers and sisters, in all the`ee other chapters around the`ee country are readied…indeed brother…power to the circle forever."

The thin man hung up the phone and lit a cigar.

...

The evening news was broadcasting a story about a missing child in Atlanta Georgia. The body of the young boy was found several days later with the major organs missing. The news did not specify the details of the child's whereabouts when the body was discovered. Moats was in shorts and a t-shirt, in the darkness of his apartment staring at his television, and frequently gazing back and forth at his front door. His pistol and badge was on the sofa next to him. He had already finished ten beers and the empty aluminum cans were stacked up on his tray table in the shape of a triangle next to several empty Chinese food cartons. Moats leaned his loaded shotgun on the sofa next to him, grabbed a letter of suspension from the Philadelphia police department and read it over again. Moats balled the suspension letter in his hand and threw it across the room. The balled-up letter struck his Marine core photo from five years earlier. Moats reached for his remote control and changed the channel on his television as he cracked another can of beer open…

...

In South Carolina a man was found hanging from a tree by his neck. The news stations and social media outlets reported the death as a suicide…there was no investigation.

The same was reported on all local news stations about a woman found hanging from a tree in Indianapolis. A suicide by hanging…

In Ohio, a young black man was shot in his back five times by a police officer who chased him. The officer stated, "The guy had a gun when I stopped him on the street." There was no weapon found at the scene or anywhere in the area…just the dead man`s cell phone.

•••

In North Carolina a doctor at a hospital was closing up the surgery on a rich white patient who had been on the kidney transplant list for a month...

In Florida, a woman smiled at her physician after he gave her the news that, after a year, her transplanted heart was doing extremely well...

At the University of Pennsylvania surgery center, two doctors were talking with a patient about her upcoming lung transplant. They assured her that the procedure would go just fine and that she would feel brand new once it was done. They ended their private consultation by saying to one another, long live, The Knights of the Golden Circle."

•••

Simmons stood proudly dressed in his white shirt, shining shoes and gloves. He received his accommodation from the chief of police. The police chief pinned captains bars on Simmons white shirt collar and assigned him to the 35th district. Simmons along with several other officers were promoted based upon their recent policing of the missing persons cases the past year.

•••

Belle Glade, Florida.

The building on Gator boulevard and East Sugar house road just off the highway was boarded up in front and appeared to be abandoned. It was painted a dull color grey, chipping paint, and was surrounded by unkept grass and overgrown weeds all around. Only the regulars from the Florida neighborhood were familiar with the building and what was inside. Several cars were parked in the rear of the building and the glass door at the rear was tinted a heavy black. A car pulled behind the building, parked and a man exited and walked to the door. He stopped and looked up at a camera mounted a few feet above the door. After a few seconds the door buzzed and the man walked inside. He strolled to the counter and waited. The inside of the waiting area was painted a shade of navy blue with mirrors covering the walls behind the front desk.

"Hello."

The man waited a few seconds and a door opened to the left of the desk and five women walked through the door dressed in cheap lingerie underwear. The man smiled and looked the women over. The women smiled and checked the man out from head to toe as they smiled pleasantries'.

The door opened again and Missy walked out dressed in a kimono style robe wearing heels and her panties. Missy strolled over to the man and kissed his face.

"Full massage, half massage, or other," Missy asked the man.

The man reached in his pocket and pulled out a roll of money.

"I want the works," the man said smiling.

Missy pointed to the women. The man chose who he wanted to spend his time with. He gave Missy a roll of money and she shoved it in her robe pocket. The man strolled to the rear of the building with his date, down a short hallway. He and the woman entered a room and shut the door…Another doorway across the small hallway opened and a different woman exited with a different man. The man smiled at Missy and the other girls as he exited the building.

"Thank you for visiting Missy`s massage parlor…come back soon," Missy said.

"A happy customer Rose? "asked Missy.

"A VERY happy customer," responded Rose smiling.

Missy smiled. She reached into her robe pocket and pulled a small baggie of heroin out and held it up in the air. Rose walked slowly toward Missy as the other women watched. Rose took the baggie and headed toward one of the empty rooms in back.

"Y`all bitches need to step it up," chastised Missy as she gazed at the remaining women.

• • •

THREE MONTHS LATER

IN TIOGA – NICETOWN

Trina, Celeste and Aminah walked the long way home from cheerleader practice. They walked down Hunting park avenue toward Broad street talking amongst one another.

"I'm hungry like…famished hungry."

The three girls shared a laugh.

"Bitch done learned a new word, famished," Aminah said teasing Trina.

"Yup…famished…I be knowing stuff."

"Let's hit the pizza shop on Broad," suggested Celeste.

"Slices on you?"

"You be knowing shit…but you aint never got money Trina."

"Bitch don't front, like I never paid for your food, never."

"Whatever jawn…level up, it's time," Celeste snapped at Trina.

The three friends walked a few more feet and Trina stopped at a phone pole and started reading a poster stapled to the pole. The poster was white with large printed black lettering on it. Across the street parked under a tree was a white mid-sized van with heavy tinted windows.

WANTED

TEENS FOR AFTER SCHOOL JOBS

EARN

$80 $90 $100 DOLLARS DAILY!!

Work evenings, and Saturdays.

FREE TRIPS and ACTIVITIES PAID FOR!!

Next to that line on the poster was a hand drawn sketch of an amusement park Farris wheel and a rollercoaster.

TRANSPORTATION PROVIDED!!!

13 years and older…BRING YOUR FRIENDS!!!

At the bottom of the poster was a numbers tab and several of the tabs were pulled off already. Trina read the poster aloud and tore off a number tab.

"Y'all gonna take one…we can all go to this job jawn together?"

"I gotta check with my dad first," Celeste responded. "I'm down though."

"It sounds too good to be true," Aminah stated. " But, I could definitely use that type paper in my life right now," Aminah added.

"I'm definitely calling this jawn as soon as I get home," Trina remarked excitedly.

Celeste and Aminah ripped tabs off the poster and put the phone numbers in their pockets. The three friends continued walking toward Broad street.

THE END.

July, 30, 2020   <u>An after word.</u>

    So much is going on in our world today. Deadly disease, protests, crooked practices in politics, murders by the hundreds in our communities, and police brutality in record numbers. When I started writing this novel, all those things were weighing heavily on my spirit. I thought about the history of African people being stripped from their homeland and stolen to the shores of a country and forced into labor for years. I thought about the thousands who sacrificed, died and bled for a country that never valued or treated them with equality, liberty or justice, all of which is decreed in the constitution that was written all those decades ago. Here we are in the 2020, with all the things that our ancestors survived, picked cotton under the lash for, fought in wars for, got lynched and Billy clubbed for, and were subjugated for, things that are still happening today, with our civil rights continuously being trampled upon, only now, in more strategic, and immoral ways. People of color are, and have been the victims of oppression in this system of injustice for far- too- long. When will it end?

    My intent while writing this work of fiction was to release some of my own anxieties about some of the things I`d witnessed happening across America. So many black people missing, hanging from trees, shot down, and suffocated by law enforcement officers, others found dead in plastic containers, some found dead with missing organs, and, in the majority of instances, there is no justice for those atrocities. The cycle of death keeps reinventing itself in this system of oppression and subjugation over and over again. My prayer is that all people of color, especially Black people in this country, get just due someday. I totally and wholeheartedly despise and abhor organizations that spew hate, death and ideals like the fictitious group in this novel. There is no place on God`s earth for groups like that, and, there has to be a way of leveling the warped playing field against such groups of hate who believe they have a right to ruin other cultures. There has to be a way of tilting the warped field in favor of those who built, sacrificed, labored, and died to make this country what it is. America should understand this, the builders of this country, if not justly rewarded for their sacrifices, will tear down the fabric, and re-build something uniquely better, that will truly be great.

    Thank you to the readers, friends, who have supported my work. I truly appreciate the love and I hope you enjoyed this novel.

    Anderson V. Bernard, peace and continued blessings.

Made in the USA
Coppell, TX
08 August 2020